ROB WILLIAMS

Cabin by the Stream

A mysterious woman steps from the woods

Rob Williams

Cabin by the Stream
**Published by Gordian Books, a division of Winged
Publications**
http://www.wingedpublications.com/

Printed in the United States of America
Revised edition: 2023

Special thanks to:
Allyson Hofer, for editorial help
Cover by: Cynthia Hickey

ISBN-13: 978-1-0881-4467-1

In dedication to my soul mate and wife,
Gwyn,
my four children, and grandchildren.
Rob Williams
August, 2020

Forward

There are times when many of us feel that our lives are possibly cursed. We experience hardships, sometimes tragedy. Most of us never see purpose behind our situations during our time on earth. As people meet others, those relationships serve to alter our lives. Sometimes those alterations are significant enough for us to realize the impacts. Others are far more subtle.

An unusual woman with no personal identification steps from the woods near John Walker's cabin by a stream and warns him that he has no right to fish on her husband's property. After John points to his cabin and insists that this is his property, the bewildered woman retreats back into the trees. Throughout this fictional mystery novel, the actual identity of the woman who claims to be Rebecca Johnson remains in question. She gives various stories regarding her past, and John's attorney/friend advises him to stay away from her. The wealthy Atlanta businessman, John, finds that he cannot force himself to abide by the attorney's advice. Within just a short period of time, John becomes inexplicably drawn to her. Follow along as John throws himself into the whirlwind life of this mysterious woman.

Chapter 1
The Woman

Glancing upward, John Walker's eyes met an unfamiliar shade of sky.

It has a pink hue. Red sky at morning, sailor take warning. I wonder if the weather is about to turn.

An unexpected eerie chill ran down his spine as he cast his fishing line into the slow running stream. The bobber on the line rose and fell with the moving water, but it was obvious to him that no fish toyed with the bait. As he reeled the line in, he heard a female voice.

"What do you think you're doing, sir?"

He turned to find a woman in a flowered pale peach dress moving in his direction from the trees. Suddenly, she stopped beside the stream bank and issued a warning.

"If you don't leave this instant, I'll call for my husband. You have no right to fish on this property."

"Seeing that I own this property, I believe that I do," he replied.

John pointed to the cabin on the edge of the

woods. The woman starred at the structure momentarily, before her eyes moved back to him. She watched John pull the night crawler off the hook and toss it into the water.

"If the weather is about to change, I should probably continue the fishing later," he stated, his eyes turning upward.

He was somewhat surprised to see that the sky had become clear blue. John fastened the hook to a guide on the fishing rod, before turning his attention back to the woman.

"I..... when did you build that cabin?" she stammered.

"About three years ago," John replied. "I love it here."

The color of her face drained; her eyes widened. She turned and quickly made her way back into the forest.

Talking about weird! She wasn't close enough for me to smell liquor, but ...what was her problem?

Just before dusk, John stepped out of the cabin to check the coals on his grill. From the porch, he spotted the woman standing near the water's edge. Her eyes met his. He raised his right hand and gave her a quick wave, but the gesture wasn't returned. Noting that the coals needed to heat for a few more minutes, he focused his thoughts on the woman.

I've never seen her before today. I have no clue why she's here. She couldn't have been hiking in that dress, so she must have a car parked on the road.

He slowly moved in her direction, studying the woman as he neared.

"Can I help you with something?" he called out.

Her wild eyes locked on his. John stopped within five feet of the woman.

"Is there a problem?" he questioned.

She turned away; her hands trembled.

"What can I do to help?" John again asked.

She took a step towards him, but no reply was given. He slowly moved closer and held out his hand. She took a step back, but then reached out. Taking her hand in his, he quietly spoke.

"Tell me what I can do to help."

Her small hands griped his. Her eyes again fixed on his, her head slightly moved back and forth.

"You seem to be somewhat distressed," observed John. "You're welcome to rest in a chair on the porch while I prepare supper. I'm about to cook something on the grill."

He released one of her hands, and gently escorted her toward the porch. Her eyes scanned the building and looked back at him. The two moved up the steps, and he led her to a Klondike chair.

"Have a seat right here," he said, releasing her hand. "I'm going inside to get the meat for the grill. I'll be right back."

"Who are you?" she finally asked, reaching for his hand again.

"I'm John Walker. What's your name?"

"Rebecca Johnson… Mrs. Rebecca Johnson."

"Can I get you a cup of coffee?"

"Thank you."

John released her hand a second time and moved

into the cabin through a screened door. He returned momentarily carrying a cup of coffee, sugar, and cream on a small wooden serving tray with legs. He placed the tray beside the chair to her right.

"I have sweetener in the cabin, it you like," he offered.

"No, you're more than hospitable."

"The coals are ready. I'm going back inside for the meat. Just relax with your coffee."

Within a couple of minutes, he returned with a plate holding two thick red steaks.

"Hungry? It's getting late, and you might feel better after a meal. You're welcome to share these with me. I plan to cook them both."

"The coffee is fine for now," she replied. "Thank you."

John dropped the two steaks on the grill and moved back up the steps.

"I need to get a few things," he said, stepping back inside the cabin.

He soon returned with a matching tray holding garlic salt, black pepper, a sauce, and metal tongs for turning the meat. Satisfied that the steaks were properly seared on one side, he turned them. He added sauce, and then the garlic salt and pepper. Turning his eyes to the woman, he saw her lips gently sipping the cup of coffee.

"It's not a special blend, just Colombian," he told her.

She gave him a polite smile.

"I guess you've noticed there's spotty cell reception out here," John stated. "It took me a while to find a carrier that gave me fair reception at the cabin. I have a land line inside, if you need to make a call."

Her hands shook as she placed the cup on the tray. Her eyes were deeply troubled, but John focused his attention back on the grill. He turned the steaks for a second time, adding the pepper and salt to the sizzling meat. When he turned back, he was started to see that she now stood beside him. A strange, unsettling sensation came over him.

Maybe she has mental or emotional problems, and off her medication. Earlier, she was on my case about fishing the stream, and now she is hanging around like an old friend. This young woman could be totally nuts.

"What's the matter?" he asked,

She silently stared at him.

"Is there someone we should call?" he asked. "You have no bag or purse. Maybe you left something in your car."

Her eyes narrowed. John's uneasy mind raced.

She says that her name is Rebecca Johnson, but she could be anybody. I'd like to see some ID on this woman. If mentally stable, she could be setting me up. There could be some guy of hers waiting at the car, waiting for dark to settle with plans to rob me. Or, maybe the two are on the run and are looking to use this cabin as a hideout.

Fear gripped his mind and soul. He thought about the pistol he kept in a drawer in the kitchen.

"As soon as the steaks are done, I'll be glad to walk you to your car," he offered. "We should at least get your purse before it turns dark. I'll get a couple of flashlights, in case they're needed on the way back. We should go before dark."

"Go?" she asked.

"Yeah. Most women hate to be without their purse."

Her hands began to shake again.

"What's going on?" he asked. "Earlier, you complained about my fishing and then walked into the woods. Why did you come back?"

"I don't know."

Her body began to shiver.

"Are you cold?"

She nodded.

"The steaks are about ready," John said. "I'll go back into the cabin for a plate, and I'll get you a coat. Would that be all right?"

She nodded.

He raced back into the cabin. He grabbed two jackets, putting on the one that held his SUV keys in a pocket. He took the loaded pistol from the kitchen drawer and placed it in the other pocket. Taking a plate for the steaks from a cabinet, he quickly made his way back to her.

"It's a little large for you, but it should warm you up," he said, handing her the jacket.

She slipped it on, as he put the steaks on the plate.

"I forgot the flashlights. I'm going to put the steaks in the microwave to keep them warm, and I'll be right back with the flashlights."

Returning with the flashlights, he turned them on and handed her one. He opened the screen door of the cabin, inviting her inside.

"No!" she said emphatically.

"I thought we could cut through and leave out the front door," John explained.

"I don't want to go inside; I don't know you," she replied.

"Fair enough, we'll walk around from the back."

He took her hand and led her down the stone steps of the cabin. She abruptly halted, as they neared the grill.

"The road is only about fifty yards from the cabin, so your car can't be far," he said, releasing her hand.

"I don't know…" she mumbled.

"You don't know what?"

"I don't know what you are doing."

"Going to find your car, and your purse. It's almost dark, so we should be going."

Her eyes were wild with fear.

"Don't you want your purse?" John asked.

"I don't know…" she replied.

"You don't know?"

"I don't know anything."

Her eyes wide and wild, she seemed almost frantic. Suddenly, the motion detecting floodlights of the cabin flooded the yard with light. The startled woman stepped back, tripping over a small wooden bench he had earlier placed near the grill. Losing her balance, she fell and hit her head on the stone steps. The flashlight dropped from her hand.

"Are you OK?" John frantically asked.

She was motionless. John stepped closer and stood over her. He heard leaves rustle in the woods. Turning his flashlight in the direction of the sound, he saw nothing.

"Who's out there?" he bellowed.

Placing his hand on the gun in his jacket pocket, he nervously scanned the forest with the flashlight.

Seeing nothing out of the ordinary, he turned his attention back to the woman. He knelt beside her and touched her face.

"Are you all right?"

There was no movement or response. He lifted her head and saw quickly that her body was totally limp. John checked her neck for a pulse and found her heart to be slowly beating. She appeared to be unconscious.

John's emotions ran in all directions. He couldn't leave an unconscious woman on the steps of his cabin, but he wanted desperately to find her car and see if a man was waiting.

She objected to coming inside the cabin, but I can't just leave her here. I doubt she's alone; she earlier mentioned a husband. If I bring her inside, she could come to and open the door for a guy to enter and shoot me dead. If she's truly alone, she could be crazy. She might put a kitchen knife in my back!

He tried to help her sit up, but her body was limp. Her head fell to one side.

Something could be seriously wrong. A lack of medication could have cause her to become dizzy and fall. She hit the steps hard. She could need medical attention. I should call someone to check her out.

Under the floodlights, John turned off both flashlights and placed them in his jacket pocket containing his keys. He lifted her limp body in his arms and carried her up the steps and into his cabin. John laid her on a couch and turned on a table lamp.

Fearful of an accomplice, he quickly turned the lock on the door and fastened the dead bolt. John knelt beside her and felt the back of her head. A large lump had formed. Bringing his hand back, there was blood.

Checking her neck for a pulse again, her eyes blinked. She seemed disoriented.

"You're inside my cabin," informed John. "You fell onto the steps. I believe you became dizzy."

Suddenly, her body tensed. Her desperate green eyes fixed on his, she grabbed his jacket with both hands. Her lips trembled.

"Please, help me!"

Chapter 2
Night

Confused and disoriented, Rebecca clung to John's jacket. Her eyes frantically darted around the room.

"What's going on?" asked John. "How can I help?"

"I just…I'm not sure," she replied. "I just…"

With fear in her eyes, her mouth tensed.

"You don't need to be afraid," he told her.

She released a sigh. Her hands fell from his coat. He could tell she was making a conscious effort to focus on his face.

"Who…why am I here?" she whispered.

"Your head hit the stone steps when you fell, and I brought you inside the cabin," John offered. "I think you should see a doctor. There is an ER about thirty minutes away."

He helped her to stand. Assured that she was able to walk, he slowly escorted her to the garage housing his SUV. Opening the front passenger door, he offered to help her in.

"No!" she protested.

"Please let a doctor take a look at your head," he said.

"I'm fine. I don't need a doctor. I was upset while on your couch, but I am just fine now. I need fresh air."

"It would make me feel so much better for a doctor to check you out."

"I said, 'No' – and I meant it. I need to get out of here. Let me out of this room right now!"

Rebecca pushed him away, her eyes searching for a door. Spotting one, she made her way to it.

"Where will you go?"

"Anywhere, but here. I have to get fresh air."

Rebecca struggled with the locked door. John placed his right hand on hers and unlocked the door with his left.

"It's unlocked," he said. "You're free to go, but I really wish you would see a doctor."

"No!" she blurted, opening the door and stepping out into the night air.

John silently watched her walk up the long drive leading to the road. Still visible in the moonlight, she left the drive and made her way into the woods beside the cabin. John reached into the pocket of his jacket to make sure he still had the flashlights, then followed from a distance. Concerned that he might startle her with the flashlight, he struggled to track her in the dark. Thankful that Fall had removed leaves from branches, he cautiously made his way through the forest. John heard a muffled sound and followed it. He found her sitting on an ancient stone foundation of a house that once stood on that site. She was audibly weeping.

"Please come back to the cabin," he offered, now turning on the flashlight. "You can't stay out here during the night."

"It's not right; I don't really know you," she replied, her swollen eyes looking up.

"Please."

"No!"

"You earlier mentioned a husband. I should give you a ride home. Is it far?"

"My home and my husband are none of your concern."

"I would think he'd be worried if you didn't return home overnight."

I told you that the matter isn't a concern of yours," Rebecca scolded.

"Do you have children?"

"Now, you've begun to pry. Stop!"

"Would you, at least, allow me to bring you a blanket? It's getting cool. I'm worried about you."

She wiped the tears with both hands. Her head dropped, and she released a sigh.

"A blanket would be welcomed," Rebecca answered.

"You shouldn't be out here in the dark," John said, turning on both flashlights. "Take this one. I'll be right back. Promise me that you won't run off while I get that blanket."

"Thank you. I won't."

Within a few minutes, John returned with a battery-operated lantern, a sleeping bag, and a hiking tent. Hanging the lantern from a broken tree limb, he began preparing a place for the tent. He removed fallen limbs and gathered fallen leaves in a pile. Rebecca watched in silence. He popped open the tent and placed it on the leaves. John unrolled the sleeping bag, unzipped it part way, and placed it in the tent.

"Now, that's better," he said, pointing to the tent. "I'm leaving you the lantern for the night. Crawl into the tent and get inside that bag. It's good for ten degrees. You should stay warm."

He removed the lantern from the tree limb and showed her how it operated.

"You didn't have to do this," Rebecca whispered.

"Yes, I did. You refused to see a doctor, and this is the least I could do. I'm worried about you."

She silently took the lantern and entered the tent.

"I hope you sleep well," John wished.

"Goodnight," she replied.

"I plan to sleep on the couch tonight. If you change your mind about seeing a doctor, or if you need anything, just knock on the door. I'll hear you."

"Thank you," said the soft voice from within the tent. "You're more than kind, sir."

John considered her last words, as he made his way back to the cabin.

Sir? I can't be that much older than this woman. Why would she call me, sir? And such an odd dialect. I can't place it.

He took a blanket from a closet, and a pillow from his bed, before settling on the couch. Concerned about the liability of a woman being injured on his property, he called his attorney, Mark Fairchild. John explained the situation. Fairchild's words weren't reassuring.

"You need a witness to her refusal of medical care. Do you have a neighbor willing to be a witness?"

"I've not made friends with those in the

community, but there is a fellow who sells me firewood from time to time," answered John.

"Call him; offer him money, if you have to," stated the attorney.

Hanging up, John immediately called Bobby Thompson. The man complained about coming over in the middle of the night when asked to stand as a witness. His tone immediately changed when John offered five hundred dollars. Bobby was there within thirty minutes. As the two approached the tent, John called out to Rebecca.

"I must interrupt your evening one more time."

The lantern burned, making the tent look like a large pale green Asian lantern.

"May I open the tent?" questioned John.

"Yes," she replied.

John unzipped tent door and introduced her to the man accompanying him. He then pulled out his cell phone and held it in front of him.

"What is happening?" she asked.

"Do you know Bobby Thompson?" John asked.

"No," she replied. "I don't see why I should be introduced to this man during the night, out here in the woods. Does he have a problem?"

"No," replied John.

"Can't this wait until morning?" she asked.

"Do you still refuse medical help?" questioned John, holding up the cell.

"Yes," she replied. "What this is about? Are you going to force me to see a doctor?"

"No, I won't force you," answered John. "Are you sure that you are well?"

"Yes," she answered, her voice showing

impatience.

"That's all," John stated. "Go back to sleep. I promise that I will not bother you again tonight."

He turned the cell in the direction of Bobby Thompson, while shining the flashlight in his direction.

"Mr. Thompson, did you hear Rebecca Johnson state that she refused my offer for medical help and that she is well?" John asked.

"Yes, I did," answered Bobby.

"Would you please take your beat session out of here and let me sleep?" the two heard her ask from inside the tent. "I thank you again, but you told me that you wouldn't bother me again tonight."

"I apologize," offered John.

With that, he zipped up the tent door and the two men made their way back to the cabin. Once there, John handed Bobby five one hundred-dollar bills from his jacket pocket.

"I believe that's about the easiest half-grand I've ever made," said Bobby. "If you wish to do this again, I'm your man."

"Thank you, but I doubt this will come up again."

"What the heck is a beat session?" asked Bobby. "I'm a good twenty years older than that woman. Is it a twenty-something saying going around on the internet?"

"I have no idea. She seems to be a unique person."

John watched Bobby drive up the drive toward the road, before partially undressing and dropping onto the couch. Hopes of putting to rest concerns about Rebecca were dashed. His alert mind wandered.

How well do I really know Bobby Thompson? The

only reason that I entered his name and number in my phone was to make sure that I had a source for firewood during the winter. He now knows that a woman is alone in a tent. She seems to be emotionally shaken, and she would be extremely vulnerable, should he decide to take advantage of her.

His eyes stared into the darkness of the room. The couch offered comfort to his tired body, but nothing helped his troubled mind. Sleep was nowhere within reach.

"Good grief," he whispered. "This weird day seems it will never end."

He retrieved a second sleeping bag from the closet and dressed himself. The glow of the flashlight cast eerie shadows among the trees, as he entered the woods. Nearing the tent, he watched for twigs on the ground.

I promised I wouldn't bother her again tonight. The sound of snapping twigs would certainly cause her concern.

He slowly unrolled the bag and placed it on the ground outside the tent. Quietly, he slid inside it. Lying in the sleeping bag, his imagination ran wild. He imagined Bobby coming back to the scene, and an ensuing confrontation between the two. His mind turned back to thoughts of a possible accomplice of Rebecca's. Images from *Easy Rider* played in his mind. The scene of someone hacking a man to death with an axe, while he slept inside a sleeping bag, was as vivid as when he first saw the movie. Exhausted, an hour later he finally fell asleep.

18

Chapter 3
A Guest

John was rudely awakened the following morning, as he felt the pressure of a shoe on his back. He turned over in his sleeping bag to find Rebecca standing over him.

"Sir, I sincerely appreciate the use of your tent last night," she said. "I've taken it down, and the sleeping bag has been rolled. I'll be leaving."

"What about breakfast?" questioned John.

"That's not your concern," she answered.

"Not a concern, simply an invitation to have breakfast at the cabin. You're a guest on my property. The least I can do is offer breakfast."

"You've shown enough kindness, sir."

"I would feel so much better to see you leave on a full stomach. Please, humor me. I insist."

"If you insist," Rebecca replied. "In return, I insist on cleaning up afterwards."

John sat up. His fit body felt sore, as he stood to his feet. The two gathered the two bags and the tent and headed through the woods to the cabin. Approaching the cabin, Rebecca broke the silence.

"You didn't have to sleep outside the tent."

"Honestly, I couldn't sleep – knowing that you were alone out in the open," John said.

"So, you're somewhat of a gentleman."

"I'm not saying that I think you're incapable of taking care of yourself. Earlier in the night, you asked for my help. So… it just made me feel better."

He dropped the tent and one bag on the back porch, and she followed in suit with the other bag.

"Do omelets sound all right?" John asked.

"I'm fine with whatever you decide to have."

"Oh, before I do anything, I have to visit the bathroom," he explained, with a grin. "The cabin has two. Let me show you the one for your use."

He turned on the guest bath light, and she poked her head inside. Her eyes scanned the wall above the toilet and found a small painting of a rustic cabin in the woods. She stepped inside for a closer look. John watched her glance at the bare wall above the painting, and then she placed her right hand on the tank of the toilet. Shaking her head, Rebecca's attention focused again on the small painting.

"This certainly isn't a painting of this cabin," she remarked.

"No, but I like the painting," John replied, smiling.

"You don't mind if I use this one?" asking for confirmation.

"That's why I showed it to you," answered John.

He gave her a silent wave of his right hand, before closing the bathroom door and going about his business. The door was still shut as he passed by it in route to the kitchen. While cutting a steak from the previous night into small pieces, he heard the muted flush.

It sounds like she's still here.

Rebecca entered the kitchen. She found him adding small pieces of steak, onions, mushrooms, and bell peppers into the beaten eggs.

"It won't take long," John promised. "Have a seat at the table by the window."

He soon presented her with a large omelet and a piece of toast, before placing an identical serving for himself on the table. He walked away, and quickly returned with two cups of coffee. As he seated himself, Rebecca spoke.

"Would you allow me to say grace?"

"Sure," John answered, bowing his head.

"We thank thee, Lord, for this our food, and we ask that you bless the hands which have prepared it. Amen."

After taking a bite of the omelet, Rebecca raised her eyes to meet John's. He watched intently, waiting for her reaction. She closed her eyes and swallowed.

"This is marvelous," she stated. "May I assume that you own a restaurant?"

"No, I've simply learned to cook a few things," John replied. "I'm glad you like it. Thank you. My parents passed away, and I inherited properties that are managed."

"Properties?"

"Stores, apartment buildings, condos, and a few office buildings," John explained.

"My word! That must keep you busy! I should be

leaving, with you having so many responsibilities."

"There's no hurry. I have people managing the properties, and they report problems or opportunities to me."

"This is a beautiful home. I should have realized… I shouldn't have bothered you. I'm sorry."

"Relax," John said, calmly. "Just relax and enjoy breakfast. I won't need to return to the city until tomorrow."

"You don't live here?"

"I split my time between here and a condo in Atlanta."

"Berries," Rebecca said, taking the last bite. "Breakfast was truly remarkable."

She stood from the table and gathered the dishes, as if she had done it a thousand times before. John watched her take them to the sink.

What an odd woman. Yet, so interesting.

John stood beside her as she began scrubbing the dishes.

"I see you have a pad and pen on the counter," she observed.

"I often need to make a list, and I like to have it handy. Most people just make a list on a cell phone, but I guess it's a habit I retained from my parents. They always had a pad and pen for notes."

"I'm sure you miss them."

"What about your husband?" he asked.

"What do you mean?" she responded, focused on the task at hand.

"I've told you about my business. What do you and your husband do? You mentioned him yesterday."

"We certainly aren't people of means, as you,"

she replied. "But we farm, and we have plenty."

"I'm sure that he's worried about you. Did you call him last night?"

She turned and gave him a look that let him know that he had pried into personal matters. She dried a cup with a dish towel, and silently placed it on the counter.

"I apologize," said John. "That's none of my business. Let me help you dry."

In silence, she washed and John dried.

"Why did you insist on staying near those ruins in the woods," John asked.

"A house once stood there which belonged to members of my family. I felt more comfortable in a familiar place."

"The paperwork for the purchase of this land didn't mention a Johnson, so would your maiden name be Alderman?" asked John.

Rebecca said nothing.

"Alderman was listed on the paperwork," he continued. "I had someone handle the purchase for me."

"Someone else handled the purchase of this property," observed Rebecca. "You have people to manage your other properties for you. What exactly do you do?"

"I make major decisions," he answered.

"I'm sorry," she apologized. "I shouldn't have asked that of you. You've been very kind to me, and I've stepped out of my place to question you."

"Stepped out of your place? What's with that? You're welcome to question me. I'm no king. I simply asked about this property once being in your family."

"I don't mean to be rude, but I don't wish to discuss it," she stated. "I'm sorry. I should leave now."

They stood in silence. She turned from him and began walking slowly toward the back door.

"Listen, I'd like to take a quick shower and then give you a ride home," John offered.

His voice seemed to echo in the stillness of the moment.

"That won't be necessary," she softly replied.

"Please wait and let me take you home. I have several errands to do today, so I'll be out anyway."

She didn't argue, but stood in silence. John made his way to his bedroom, quickly showered and dressed. Returning to the kitchen, he found a note on the table. It read:

Thank you, for your graciousness.

John marveled at the perfection of cursive script. Every lower-case letter was the same height, width, and style. The larger capital letter was flowing with elegance.

"It's a thing of beauty," he mumbled. "It's almost a piece of art."

It's obvious that she and her husband are having a fight. It would be stupid to involve myself, but I can't help being concerned.

This was unlike John, to consider meddling in the affairs of others. Life was easy for him. There was no parental care, because they had both passed away. He had no wife or children, to tie him down or cause him worry. John enjoyed the temporary caresses of shallow women, drawn to his riches. But, not here at the cabin. It was a retreat from games with money-hungry women and confrontational business meetings in the city. The cabin was a place of peace…until now.

Chapter 4
The Cafe

John closed his laptop. He found it impossible to concentrate on the financial reports emailed to him. Thoughts of Rebecca Johnson crowded his mind.

One moment she seems to be stable, but other forms of her behavior are simply odd. I'm not convinced that the blow to her head wasn't significant.

He slipped on a jacket and made his way out of the cabin. Standing beside the forest, he listened for sounds of rustling leaves. Nothing. The fall wind was perfectly still; no creaking of swaying branches; no person or critter caused the crunching of twigs or leaves. Soon, only the leaves beneath his feet rustled as he walked through the woods.

He reached the ruins of the home Rebecca claimed to have been in her family. He studied the trees growing in the center of the abandoned stone foundation before walking the perimeter, searching for evidence that she had been there. He found no signs of her. John glanced at the time displayed on his cell.

It's a long walk, but maybe she went into Hatchett. She probably has relatives in the area. I need to handle a few things before departing for Atlanta.

In route to the small community, John spotted Rebecca standing in a cemetery next to St. Paul Methodist Church. He was surprised that this little building was still in operation, being over a hundred years old. She had walked just over a mile from the cabin. John parked his vehicle. As he approached the younger woman, she was visibly weeping. He called out to her.

"Are you all, right?"

Rebecca wiped her face with her hands. He touched her shoulder, while glancing down at a grave. She was standing at the tombstone of Lilly Johnson, an infant who died April 1921.

"Are you related to the child buried here?" he asked.

"Yes."

"How so?"

Rebecca slowly walked away, still rubbing her eyes. Catching her by the arm, John asked her why she was so upset.

"So many graves, for such a small church," she whispered.

"I'm on my way to Hatchett. Can I offer you a ride?"

"No sir. But, thank you. You've done enough."

John's cell rang. He stepped aside to answer the call from a manager in Atlanta. Turning back to her direction after the short call, he watched Rebecca step from the grass of the cemetery and onto the road leading to Hatchett. Jogging, he caught up with her.

"Did I offend you, in some way?" he asked.

"No. It's time to part ways. You have business to attend to, and I have things to do."

"The call…my meeting in Atlanta has been moved to tomorrow. There's no rush. I certainly have time to give you a lift."

"No sir."

Her eyes, still puffy from weeping, were locked on his. It was apparent to him that she was sincere, and that she wanted the conversation to end.

"All right," he replied.

John returned to his SUV. He placed the key in the ignition and watched in silence as she deliberately made her way on foot along the road.

What is it about this woman? She is driving me nuts.

Baffled by her behavior, he returned to the cabin. From there, John called his attorney to inform him of the captured conversation during the night and that she was no longer on the property.

"You should count yourself fortunate that she is gone," replied Fairchild.

"What if the head wound is more serious than it seems?" asked John.

"You have the recording, proving her rejection of medical treatment. You're in the clear, now. Relax."

After the call ended, John thought about the advice to relax. He was somewhat relieved to know that there were no grounds for a lawsuit, but relaxation was nowhere in sight. His nerves were on edge. He was consumed with the welfare of Rebecca Johnson.

What is wrong with me? This not me. I don't do this!

Two hours later, John received a call from Bobby Thompson.

"Your little lady is causing concern in Hatchett," complained Bobby. "I just got off the phone with Sally Perkins. You know…she owns Sally's Café. She told me that a woman named Rebecca Johnson had inquired about a job as cook at her place. The woman had no ID, but said that she was acquainted with John Walker."

"Good grief," said John. "Why did Ms. Perkins call you?"

"I told her about selling you firewood, and she figured that I had your number. I said that I would let you know."

"I'm not really responsible for Rebecca Johnson."

"I know that. I'm just telling you that there is a situation, and your name is being battered around."

"I'm not sure what I can do about it."

"Mr. Walker, you have to know that you're already the talk of Hatchett. It's unusual for a very wealthy owner of an Atlanta business to buy property here. You stay bottled up in that cabin like a hermit, and that has gossip flowing like Niagara Falls."

"Hermit? I've eaten at Sally's Café. I'm no hermit. I'm busy, and this place offers me some relaxation and peace of mind."

"Sally doesn't have peace of mind right now," replied Bobby. "She doesn't know what to do with a person without any identification."

"Is Rebecca still at the café?"

"Yeah. She started crying, so Sally told her that

she should go home. The woman went outside, and immediately scurried into the alley beside the café. Sally waited a few minutes, and then followed her there. The girl was still crying. Sally's a kind soul. She brought her back in and let her sit at the table on back left side. She gave her a cup of coffee, then called me."

"All right, I'm on my way. Thanks for the call."

John stared out a rear window of the cabin. The gentle stream painted a picture of beauty and peace, but he felt none of it. He reached for the keys to the SUV and headed for the restaurant.

Stepping into Sally's Café, he spotted the owner behind the counter. Her gaze caused him concern.

"I'm John Walker," he announced.

"I know who you are," Sally replied. "You've been here before. I have a troubled young woman here who claims she knows you."

"I just recently meet her, and I know little about her."

"You knew her well enough to let her camp out on your property. Bobby told me about being called in the middle of the night."

"It's not like that."

"You two are adults, and that's none of my business."

"She was there for just one night. I don't know where she lives. She just appeared out of nowhere and hung around. I tried to get her to let me get her help, but she insisted on staying in those woods."

"Like I said, it's not my business. It is my business when someone with no identification comes asking for employment."

"I had no idea that she had none," said John. "She

seems to be a little lost. Is she here?"

"Around the corner, sitting at one of the back tables. She said that her name is Rebecca Johnson."

As John started in her direction he was stopped by Sally.

"No wait!" she warned. "There's more."

"What?"

"When I asked for driver's license or social security number, she had no paperwork. I told her that the documentation was required for employment. She seemed OK until she picked up a newspaper from the counter."

"What do you mean?" asked John.

"The young lady burst into tears. It was like she was having some kind of panic attack. She slammed it back onto the counter, and just freaked out. It was flat weird!"

"I should talk to her," John suggested.

"I think maybe she has mental problems. You say that you really don't know her?"

"No, she was a little disturbed when I met her. But she calmed down. I really don't know much more than you do."

"Do you think she escaped from a facility? Like a mental hospital, or something?"

"I don't think so," answered John. "I'll talk with her."

Stepping around the wall, he saw Rebecca sitting at the table sipping a cup of coffee. As he neared her, he softly called out.

"Rebecca."

She glanced in his direction, but said nothing. Her face appeared worn; her shoulders bent forward.

"May I sit with you?" he asked.

She nodded.

"Are you all right?" John pressed.

"I don't know," she whispered.

John sat across from her and reached out his right hand. She took it.

"Can you help me?" she pleaded, in a whisper.

"Is it your husband? Did he hurt you?"

"No – never...." she replied.

Taking his cell phone from his left jacket pocket, he slid it over to her.

"Call him," John said. "I'll stay with you and make sure that you're safe."

"I can't."

"Sure, you can," John reassured. "Tell him that he must leave the farm and come talk."

"You don't understand."

"You're probably right, but I'll stay here with you. If he's abusive, it's best that you meet in public. Take the cell and give him a call."

John picked up the cell phone from the table and attempted to hand it to her.

"I'm sorry. I don't know what that thing is, or how to use it," she stammered.

"You've not used a cell phone?"

"No," she replied.

John slowly brought the cell back. He studied the young woman sitting across from him.

"Well, give me the number," he offered. "I'll call him."

"I have something to tell you," Rebecca said.

Her eyes were filled with a combination of fear and confusion. She reminded John of a lost child at a carnival; a frightened little girl, separated from her parents. Her lips trembled.

"I no longer have a farm," she said. "I have nothing."

"Are you saying that you and your husband are homeless?" asked John. "What can I do to help?"

"I'm not sure if anyone can help."

"I have resources. But first, I think we need to contact your husband."

"You can't contact him. My husband is dead."

Chapter 5
A Deal

"**Dead?**" **John asked**. "Dead? What happened?"

"He was a good man," Rebecca replied. "That's all I intend to say."

"I assumed you were staying away from your husband because of a fight between the two of you."

"I don't belong here. I want to leave this place."

"You said that you have no home. Where would you go?"

Without saying another word, Rebecca rose from the table and started for the door. Baffled, John followed. He caught up with her just outside the café.

"What are you going to do?" he asked.

"I don't know."

"I want to help."

"I'm not your problem; I've caused you enough trouble. I'll manage."

"You have no identification, and I would guess that you have no money. Without papers, you have little chance of employment. Why don't you have identification papers?"

"I just don't. I've never needed them before."

"Have you ever worked for an employer?"

"Sir, my situation shouldn't be your concern."

"On a temporary basis, would you work for me as a housekeeper at my cabin?" John offered.

The words came out of his mouth before he could stop them. She seemed surprised, and he was completely shocked by his own proposal.

I must be out of my mind. What's wrong with me?

"That's very kind of you, sir," she answered.

"What do you say?" John continued.

"I would only need room and board," she said,

"Absolutely, not. How do you plan to better your situation without money? I said that this offer is temporary. I don't imagine the work to be more than a couple of hours each day, and I'll pay you fifteen dollars per hour."

"I'm not that kind of woman!" Rebecca exclaimed. "Just forget it!"

She stormed off, heading for the road. John caught her by the arm.

"You misunderstand," he said.

Rebecca angrily pulled her arm from his hand.

"I believe that I do. You plan to take advantage of a widow. I would rather starve!"

"Stop! Give me an opportunity to explain. I'm currently paying five hundred dollars each month for a cleaning service. I live alone. I'm often in Atlanta, so I really don't make that much of a mess. You would have Saturdays and Sundays off, and I think the work would only require a couple of hours each day during the week. It's very comparable to what I now pay."

"You pay a cleaning service five hundred dollars a month?" Rebecca stammered.

"The cleaning company is in Taccoa. The crew has a long drive to reach this cabin. By the time the work is done, the effort takes the majority of a workday."

"Why aren't you paying a local person?" Rebecca asked.

"I have my reasons, and I can afford it."

"It's really none of my business. I apologize for asking."

"I want to do this," John stated emphatically. "I don't know if God or fate exist, but I'm beginning to think that I'm supposed to help you find a resolution to your situation."

"You are talking about paying me thirty dollars per day for two hours of work?" asked Rebecca. That's pure kibosh!"

"So, how much work should you do for thirty dollars?" asked John. "What seems right to you?"

"I can't imagine. If I scrubbed every inch of your cabin each week, cooked all your meals, cleaned up, washed and ironed all of your clothes... that couldn't possibly add up to one hundred and fifty dollars per week."

"It's a deal!" John exclaimed, holding out his hand.

"Applesauce!" she exclaimed. She turned to walk away.

"I've got money, and you certainly need some," John called out. "Believe me, I can afford what I'm offering. I'm giving you an opportunity."

"Something's not right," she said, turning back.

"I think it's a good deal for me," he replied. "I'm currently paying that much, just for the cleaning."

"It's your money," she said. "But just temporarily. I won't take advantage of your generosity for very long. I promise."

"Are you going to shake my hand?" John asked, his hand still extended.

"Yes, sir," she said, taking his hand.

"Great! I'll drive you back to the cabin."

He opened the passenger door of his SUV and pointed to the leather seat. Rebecca took hold of the seat and awkwardly pulled herself into a seated position. John took his seat behind the wheel.

"You have to put the seat belt on; it's the law," he advised.

Rebecca starred at him.

"I'm sorry," she whispered.

"It's at your right shoulder," he explained. "Just pull it across your body and fasten the clip right here."

She turned and took both portions of the nylon belt in her hand and pulled unsuccessfully.

"I'm unable to pull it free," Rebecca said, embarrassed.

John reached over her and pulled on the single portion containing the clip, he quickly snapped it into position. While leaning over her, his nose picked up a slight scent of body odor.

Of course. She seems to have only the clothes on her back, and it's anybody's guess as to when she's had an opportunity to bathe.

He started the engine and backed away from the café. Her body stiffened, as he started down the road in the direction of the cabin.

"So, you can do math," he said.

"What?"

"You quickly calculated that thirty dollars per weekday equated to one hundred fifty dollars each week," John explained.

"I'm not stupid."

"I know little about you, but I don't consider you to be stupid. Your name is Rebecca Johnson, you're a widow who has lost her property, and I know that you are somewhat educated. That's a start."

"I don't need an education to scrub floors, and that's what I'll be doing for you," Rebecca snapped.

"True, but I hope you won't be spending your life scrubbing floors. I think you're capable of more than that."

He glanced down at her pale hands, clutching the leather seat.

"Are you all right?" he asked.

"Will you please slow down?"

"Sure," he replied. "I'm driving the speed limit, but I can drive slower if you wish."

"Please."

"Is this better?" John asked.

"Thank you, sir."

"You said that you once had a farm. Where was it?"

"Not far from here," she answered.

"Can you be more specific?"

"You would never be able to find it."

"I have GPS. We should be able to find it."

"Why is that important?" she questioned. "My parents and my husband have passed away. There is no one around for you to speak with. I'm alone."

"Put yourself in my position," John said. "Wouldn't you want to know more about an employee?"

"I understand, but I can't help you," she answered.

"Once we reach the cabin, I plan to call my attorney. I need advice as to what I can do to help you obtain paperwork."

"What kind of paperwork do I need?"

"A birth certificate would be a start. What was the hospital of your birth?"

"I was a healthy baby; I didn't need a hospital," Rebecca answered. "I was born at home."

"Do you have the name of a midwife?" John pressed.

"No," Rebecca answered. "I told you that I know of no one who can give you information about me."

"You must have gone to school, and a school would have records," he suggested.

"No!"

John pulled the SUV in front of the garage door of the cabin and reached into the console for the remote. She watched intently, as he pressed the button that caused the door to raise.

"You have all kinds of gadgets, don't you?" she asked. "I think that someone of your wealth would have a driver."

"I like to drive. Maybe I like to be in control."

John pulled the vehicle into the garage and lowered the door behind them. He turned off the ignition and took a deep breath.

"My attorney is probably going to be frustrated

with me," he said. "He earlier advised me to rid myself of you."

"Why didn't you heed his advice?" Rebecca softly asked.

"Beats the heck out of me. He'll get over it. I pay him well, to keep him on retainer."

"You pay a lawyer a lot of money, and then ignore his advice?"

"I told you that I like to be in control."

He escorted Rebecca into the cabin and showed her the second bedroom.

"It doesn't have its own bath, so you'll have to use the main one," he explained.

"It's truly luxurious. Thank you, sir. I'll begin by cleaning this bathroom."

"You'll begin by taking care of yourself today. Until I purchase work uniforms for you, I expect you to begin work in clean clothes. For today, I want you to take a bath and wash your clothes."

John marched off to his bedroom and returned carrying several items.

"I store things in case I should have an unexpected guest," he stated. "These are yours. This bathrobe is still in the plastic bag provided by the cleaners, and here is a towel and a wash rag for your bath."

"You are very kind," she said, taking the items.

"I suggest that you use the bathrobe while you wash your clothes, and then just relax a while in the bathtub…or take a shower if you wish. In the bathroom, you'll find a visitor's kit in the first drawer on the left. It contains toothpaste, a toothbrush, a hairbrush, a small bottle of mouth wash, and a couple of disposable razors. I want you to take this opportunity to clean up and relax today. Tomorrow will be another day."

"Yes, sir."

She made her way to the main bathroom. Within five minutes, she came into the kitchen wearing the bathrobe and carrying her clothes. John watched as she placed the drain mechanism in the sink and began to run warm water.

"I have a washer and dryer," he said, turning off the water.

"What?"

"Come here."

He opened a pair of French doors to reveal a washer and dryer.

"I don't know…" whispered Rebecca. "Would you mind if I wash my clothes in the sink?"

"You are welcome to wash them however you wish," he answered. "I get it. Some garments are to be washed by hand. I shouldn't have second guessed you. The bottle by the sink contains soap. I think it should work for your clothes."

"Sir, is there a line?"

"A line?"

"A line to dry the clothes," she explained.

"There is a delicate setting on the dryer," John said.

"Please. I want to hang them to dry."

"I'm sorry… hey, I have an idea. I have a ball of nylon twine. I could tie the twine between the posts of the back porch. Would that work?"

"Perfectly, sir!" she replied, with a smile.

She proceeded to wash her flowered dress in the sink. John watched intently, as she scrubbed it and her undergarments between the knuckles of her small hands. After a few minutes, he excused himself and quickly moved to the back porch. Within just a few minutes, a line for the clothes was tied between the posts.

Returning to the great room, John took a seat in his favorite leather chair and picked up a magazine. Instead of the bathrobe, he imagined her in an attractive maid uniform. There was something indescribably satisfying about the moment.

Rebecca tightly squeezed the water from each garment. Soon, she stood in front of him holding the damp clothes.

"The line?" John asked.

He proudly showed her the line on the back porch, and then returned to the chair and magazine. Once she finished hanging the clothes over the line, John watched her gracefully move toward the main bathroom.

"There are bottles of shampoo and conditioner for your hair on the back corners of the tub," John offered.

"Thank you," she replied, closing the door.

John was unable to concentrate on the magazine.

I need answers.

Once he heard the water begin to fill the tub, he left the chair and made his way to the back porch. He awkwardly fumbled at her clothes on the line, looking for clues. John was astounded to find a lacy slip and thigh high stockings draped across the line. Oddly shaped cotton panties appeared to be twice the size needed for a woman of her figure. John found no tag on the dress.

Are these hand-made?

John stealthily returned to the chair and magazine.

Rebecca returned to the bedroom, and John considered rewording the sponsorship letter to match her wishes. He felt the vibration of his cell phone in his pocket.

"Hello," answered John.

"Hey this Bobby Thompson. I heard you hired that woman to be your live-in maid."

"Did you call to confirm gossip?"

"No. I just remembered something that might interest you."

"What might that be?"

"My Daddy was hunting back up in the mountains about fifteen years ago, and he stumbled on a group of hippie families living in tee-pees."

"Why would this interest me?"

"I thought maybe that woman with no ID had come out of the mountains. Maybe she was part of that group."

Silence.

"Are you still there, Mr. Walker?"

"I'm here," said John. "Do you think your father would be able to find this group again?"

"No, his mind's no good now. He's got a bad case of old-timers. He doesn't even recognize me anymore."

"I'm sorry to hear that he suffers from Alzheimer's, Bobby. Do you remember anything about the group?"

"He said the leader of the bunch was a Viet Nam veteran. They lived off the land and moved their teepees around. There's no telling if they are even up there anymore. I just thought it might be possible that she came from those people."

"Thanks for the call," replied John.

John placed the copy of the letter on an end table

near the chair. Seated there, he thought about the remoteness of nearby mountains of northeast Georgia and formed a hypothesis.

She didn't know what to do with the seat belt of the SUV, and she seemed unaccustomed to riding in vehicles. It's very possible that she lived her life in an ultra-conservative cult, somewhere up in those mountains. She could have been born at home, homeschooled, and forced to wear those modest handmade clothes. Maybe sickness spread throughout the cult, killing her husband and her parents. I doubt they would have advanced medicine. Or perhaps she decided to rid herself of this oppressive group and simply escaped. The theory offers a logical explanation as to why she has no identification papers. Rebecca is intelligent. My bet is that she escaped.

Chapter 6
The Letter

John placed a call to his attorney, Mark Fairchild. He explained the situation and offered the theory about the backwoods cult.

"What are you freaking doing?" barked Fairchild. "Why in the world did you bring this woman into your home? This isn't even like you!"

"For some strange reason, I feel that I'm supposed to give her help," said John.

"You FEEL like…" replied Fairchild. "Feel? Are you listening to yourself? Are you OK?"

"Yeah, I'm fine. Do you have suggestions regarding what to do about her lack of paperwork?"

"I gave you advice, and you've completely ignored it. Don't you see her lack of paperwork as a red flag?"

"I get that. I really do. However, I think I should help this person. I'll pay you over and above the retainer to work on this. What can be done for her?"

"It's not my area of expertise, but I'll look into

it," promised the frustrated attorney.

"Thank you, Mark."

Rebecca entered the room wearing the robe and sat on the chair opposite John.

"My clothes are still a little damp," she said.

"I've asked my attorney to look into what can be done to help you obtain paperwork," explained John. "You'll never be able to move on to other employment without it."

"Thank you, sir."

Her grateful eyes left his. Her mind seemed to distance itself from the conversation. John watched her silently pull the brush through her wet hair.

———•●•———

"She would need to prove citizenship or fill out an Affidavit for US citizenship using a US Department of State form," Mark Fairchild explained that evening on a call to John.

"So, that's it?" asked John. "She needs to fill out paperwork?"

"You said that she has no proof of citizenship, so she may need a sponsor," the attorney answered. "She has no legal paperwork supporting her claim to citizenship, and she must provide convincing rationale as to why she has none. She must have compelling evidence of some kind. In my opinion, the explanation you gave me seems to be a stretch."

"What would a sponsor need to do?"

"You really don't know this woman. I'm advising you to step away from this and send her on her way."

"I told her that I would give her a temporary job

until she has paperwork. How hard could it be to act as a   sponsor?

"You could write a letter of support, vouching for the credibility of the cult story," stated Mark. "Your public standing and your wealth might ensure that she would not become a burden on the state. There's a possibility that it could go forward. As your legal advisor, and as a friend, I'm telling you to leave this alone. It could very well result in damaging your credibility. I advise against taking the risk."

"What could it hurt?" asked John.

"For all you know, this woman could be on the run from the law," said Mark. "Have you considered this as a possibility? She could have purposely ditched her identification. You would be considered an accomplice to whatever she is up to. She could be playing you."

"I don't think so.

"You understand that you aren't supposed to hire someone without paperwork. This would be like hiring someone who illegally came over the border from Mexico."

"Like that doesn't happen all the time? Besides, she's not from Mexico. I'll be in Atlanta tomorrow. You can meet her yourself."

John ended the call. Sitting at the kitchen table, he penned a letter. Afterwards, he gently knocked on the door of the bedroom he had earlier assigned to Rebecca. She came to the door wearing the robe.

"We need to talk," explained John. "If you don't mind, please come out to the main room."

"Yes, sir."

The two seated themselves.

"Where are your clothes?" John asked.

"I found hangers in the closet. I undressed for the night. I hope you don't mind."

"That's fine. I've had a couple of discussions with my attorney. The only way that I can legally hire you is for you to be in the process of obtaining identification papers. You'll need to fill out forms, and I may need to act as your sponsor."

"I can't ask you to do that," Rebecca said. "I won't hold you to the agreement about being your housekeeper. If you will permit me to sleep here tonight, I'll leave in the morning."

"That's not needed. I'll help you with the paperwork and I'm willing to act as your sponsor."

"Thank you, sir. I'm grateful."

"You'll need to come with me to Atlanta tomorrow to meet with my attorney. It was obvious that you were nervous while riding with me today, but you'll have to do a few things which will allow me to help you."

"I'm sorry that I complained about the speed," she said.

"First, I must ask you something," John stated. "Are you a US citizen?"

"Yes, I'm very proud to be an American citizen," she answered.

"I've written this letter to support that claim, explaining your situation. I want you to read it over and sign at the bottom."

Rebecca took the letter from his hand and began to read. She suddenly handed it back to him.

"What gave you the idea that my family were members of some religious cult group, and that they kept me from society?" she shouted.

"Do you have a better explanation for your situation?" asked John.

"I don't want my family involved!" she exclaimed.

"I don't know if you appreciate the mess that you're in," explained John. "You must have a reasonable explanation as to why you have no identification papers."

"Papers, papers, papers! That's all people want to talk about around here."

"Regardless of where you lived in the past, identification papers are required to do anything in this world," John said. "I'm trying to help you. You have to help yourself."

"Aggghh!" exclaimed Rebecca.

"Start talking. I'm sticking my neck out for you, and against the advice of counsel. Be honest with me. Do you have a better explanation as to why you don't have identification papers?"

"No," answered Rebecca. "No, I don't."

"Are you in trouble with the law?" asked John. "Be honest. You owe me that much. I'm not going to turn you in."

"I'm not in trouble with the law; I promise."

"Unless you can provide a better explanation of your situation, this is your only shot. Will you sign this?"

"I didn't escape from my family," she said. "My family members passed away, and I'm here alone. That's the honest truth."

"I'll rewrite the letter to state that your family members died, and that you made your way to this property," said John. "Will you sign that letter of explanation?"

"Is this the only option that I have?"

"It's the only one that I see," said John.

"I'll sign it. I know that you're trying to help me. I just hate having to prove that I'm an American."

"Try to get some sleep. I'll rewrite the letter, and we'll take it with us to see Mark Fairchild tomorrow at 10:00 AM in Atlanta. I have a business meeting at 1:00 PM, so we will have a full day."

"I honestly think that God led me to you," she said. "You've gone out of your way to help me. I could have fallen into evil hands. I'm grateful to have found a man with a kind soul."

"I wouldn't go that far. I'm no angel."

She turned and headed back to the bedroom. John watched the movements of her body under the white robe.

She can't be that innocent.

Chapter 7
Legalities

"**We'll have to** travel faster than we did on the road yesterday," warned John. "Try to relax. I've driven these highways hundreds of times."

He watched her fasten the seat belt on her own for the first time. He increased speed gradually as they moved down the rural road.

"There will be several of these roads before we reach Interstate eighty-five," he told her.

"What's an interstate?" she asked.

"I suspected it would be unfamiliar to you. It's major highway that's much straighter, smoother, and larger than these county roads. We'll travel faster on the interstate."

Rebecca nodded. Within minutes her grip on the seat relaxed.

"Do you like music?" John asked.

"Yes," she replied.

John reached into the console and pulled out a CD. Her eyes were fixed on the item. He slid it into the player and adjusted the volume.

"This is a recording of Craig Ogden, playing a classical guitar," explained John.

"Your gadgets never cease to amaze me!" she exclaimed. "Where is the sound coming from?"

John pointed to a few of the front speakers.

"That's the oddest phonograph record I've ever seen," observed Rebeca. "It's so small, yet the sound is so clear."

"It's called a compact disc, or a CD for short."

"This is beautiful," she said, closing her eyes.

Her breathing slowed. Within minutes her hands left the seat she had been griping. Rebecca opened her eyes and silently watched the passing scenery. She smiled and turned to John when the CD started again on the first track.

"Do you want to hear this again, or would you like to listen to a different CD?" John asked.

"Do you have something of someone singing?"

He replaced the Ogden CD with one of Josh Groban. Again, she closed her eyes. After the third song, she made another request.

"Do you have one of someone singing and playing a guitar?"

"This is one by Eric Clapton, called *Unplugged*," he said. "I think you may like it. However, there is a sad song about his little boy who died. Do you want to hear it?"

"Yes."

He pushed a button several times until it reached the mentioned track. Within seconds, tears streamed down Rebecca's cheeks. He reached into the glovebox and presented her with a small box of tissues.

"That's one of the saddest songs I've ever heard," she said, drying her cheeks and dabbing her nose. "Are all the songs sad?"

"The style of music is called *the blues*, but not all are this sad. Would you like to hear the rest?"

Rebecca nodded and closed her eyes.

John interrupted her listening with the announcement that they were turning onto the ramp leading to the interstate. Again, he increased speed until they reached sixty-five miles per hour. Her small hands again gripped the seat. Over the next five miles, he inched the vehicle upward until they reached the speed limit.

"Gracious!" she blurted. "How fast are we traveling?"

"Seventy miles per hour."

"I would have never guessed a vehicle could travel this fast, and there are other automobiles moving even faster. Why is everyone in such a hurry?"

———•●•———

Rebecca seemed astounded at the sight of the tall buildings in north Atlanta. John explained that some of the buildings near his condo in the Buckhead Business District were larger.

"I've seen photographs of New York city," Rebecca stated. "If I had not seen the Atlanta road sign, I would have guessed we were in New York."

John parked the SUV in the parking deck attached to the office building used by his attorney. The two walked briskly until they reached the elevator. Once they entered the suite of Mark Fairchild, his administrative assistant ushered them into the office.

"This is Rebecca Johnson," introduced John. "My attorney, Mark Fairchild."

"Ms. Johnson," welcomed Mark, extending his hand.

"So, you want to go through with this?" the attorney asked John.

"Yes."

"Will you both take a seat in front of my desk?" the attorney offered.

"Mr. Walker is making an extraordinary effort on your behalf," Mark said to Rebecca. "I certainly hope that it goes well for you both."

"I'm grateful," replied Rebecca.

Mark motioned to his administrative assistant to present the affidavit paperwork.

"I'm willing to complete the form, and have you sign it afterwards," explained Mark. "My administrative assistant will place the Notary Public seal, making this an official document. Let's begin with your age."

"I'm twenty-six years old," said Rebecca.

"Birthday?"

"August twelfth."

Mark wrote "08/12/1993" on the form.

He asked her place of birth, and she gave him the same county in northeast Georgia as John's cabin. When he asked for the birthdays of her parents, she told him that she didn't know that information. She offered that her father, Alvin Smith, was twenty-two and her mother, Lulu May Anderson, was nineteen when she was born. After a discussion, they estimated years and months for each.

"I never knew my grandparents," Rebecca added.

"I explained to Mr. Walker that I have no living relatives."

"Your name is Johnson," stated Mark. "Tell me about your husband."

"Grady passed away," replied Rebecca. "We were married for about three years."

"I'm sorry to hear of your loss," consoled the attorney. "What about your children?"

"I lost a child at birth," she said. "As I told John, I have no one. Everyone is now dead."

"Again, I'm sorry for your loss," Mark remarked. "This puzzles me. Your husband and parents, all of your family members are now dead?"

"Yes."

"Can you explain?" Mark asked.

"I don't want to talk about it."

"Wouldn't you be curious if I told you that every member of my family was now dead?" asked Mark.

"They're all dead! All of them. There is nothing that anyone can do about it."

"Were they murdered?" asked Mark.

"No!" she exclaimed.

Her eyes wildly glared at John.

"Do I have to go through all of this?" she asked her sponsor. "Why do I have to be badgered?"

"Mr. Walker is your sponsor, but I am handling the paperwork for you," explained the attorney. "You need to provide me with as much information as you can."

"What do you want from me?" she whispered.

"Did your family die of natural causes?" asked Mark.

"Yes."

"Everyone?" questioned the attorney.

"I don't know why my baby died. She looked perfect. The cord wasn't around her neck. I felt her kick the day before I gave birth. She was beautiful, but she never took a breath. I don't have an answer for you."

"I don't mean to cause you pain," Mark said. "I'll submit what we have and see what happens."

"Can we just go back?" she softly asked John.

"You'll need to sign the form," he replied.

Rebecca signed the form. The administrative assistant had her repeat an oath to the validity of the information on the affidavit and in the letter written by John, and then stamped both documents. She took a digital photo of Rebecca with a cell phone.

"John, I'll submit the paperwork and let you know of the outcome," promised the attorney. "I can't guarantee anything," he said, facing Rebecca.

"Thanks, Mark," said John.

The Administrative Assistant ushered them into the empty hall. As the door of the office closed, Rebecca turned to John.

"Do you think God is punishing me?"

Her eyes were filled with tears. Though the paperwork was about to be submitted on her behalf, she seemed broken and weary.

"I'm not a priest," John answered. "I wouldn't begin to know if God punishes. Why would you think that?"

"I've lost everyone I loved, and everything that I once knew to be true," she said. "What else can it be?"

"So, you believe in God?" he asked.

"Of course. I just don't seem to understand what God wants of me."

"In the place where you lived before, did you attend church?"

"Yes."

"Would you like to visit a church? Do you think that would help?"

"Yes."

"What about that church down the road from the cabin, the one with the small cemetery?"

"I'd like to go a different one?"

"So, you aren't a Methodist?"

"I want to go where no one knows me. People talk. Some of the local people probably attend that church, and they'll probably gossip about me staying with you."

"All right. We'll find one."

As the two rode the elevator to the level of the parked SUV, Rebecca's gaze seemed to be focused on an imaginary and distant world. She didn't hear the text from the attorney to John's cell phone.

"Sending the digital photo of Rebecca Johnson to the FBI and to mental facilities in north Georgia. Before you step out on this ledge, you need assurances that she isn't in criminal or mental health databases."

58

Chapter 8
Enlightenment

Rebecca's wide eyes captured every aspect of John's sixteenth floor condo in the Buckhead Business District of Atlanta. He had to coax her to a window.

"This view is amazing, but it scares me to death," she said.

"I must attend a meeting, but you should be fine here," said John. "I won't be gone long. Tonight, I would like to take you to a nearby restaurant."

"I have to stay here?" she asked. "Am I sort of a prisoner until I have papers?"

"No, you're not a prisoner."

"I'm free to go outside the building?"

"Of course. But as your sponsor, I'm taking a risk on your behalf. This is a big city, and I don't believe you're accustomed to it or the people. I hope that you would be careful, and not find yourself in trouble."

"The sun is shining. It's a beautiful day, and I may want to take a walk."

"Do you remember the man I spoke with

downstairs in the lobby?”

"Yes, he gave you a card.”

"He's called a concierge, and he gave me a guest card for you. Did you watch me place a card like it in the elevator and in the door to the apartment?”

"I watched you.”

"Take this card. It will allow you access to the elevator and the apartment door. If you have questions about anything, that man can provide you with information. This is a large city. Being unfamiliar, you could become lost. Please don't go far from this building.”

"I won't.”

Before John left for the meeting, he allowed her to practice using the guest key card on the apartment door. She thanked him and went back inside.

When John returned three hours later, Rebecca wasn't inside the apartment. He waited a half hour, before approaching the concierge in the lobby.

"I obtained a guest key from you earlier today,” John began. "A woman was with me.”

"I saw her exit the building about an hour ago,” replied the concierge.

John raced out onto the sidewalk and headed left toward a large mixed-use complex. He glanced in the windows of stores and cafes, searching for her. Soon after John started back to his apartment building, he spotted her speaking with a man. The two were standing on the corner across from him. She suddenly slapped the man hard across his face. John called out to Rebecca, and her eyes met his. She turned her attention on the man and briefly spoke to him. He looked in John's direction. Immediately, the man briskly walked away, repeatedly looking back over his shoulder at John.

"Did you know that man?" John pressed, as he reached her.

"You told me that I'm not a captive," she replied.

"Did you know him?"

"Not before today."

"Who was he?"

"Just a man."

"What did he want?"

"Why is that your business?" Rebecca asked. "Are you going to question me every time I have a conversation with someone."

"You certainly may speak with anyone you wish, but you hit the guy. What was that about?"

"I'm not a vamp," she answered.

"What"

"He insinuated things."

"Like what?

"Just forget it," she said, rolling her eyes.

"OK, I get it. Sorry. I guess I can be a little dense."

"A little?" she asked.

"Well, you certainly handled it," said John. "You had him running. I saw him looking over his should at you."

"I believe he was looking at you."

"At me?"

"I told him that you were my brother," she said, with a chuckle.

"Are you up for a little shopping?" John asked.

"Sure."

"We'll need my car."

Traveling south, the two reached a shop that sold a variety of uniforms. Rebecca was fitted, and he allowed her to select three uniforms to wear as this housekeeper.

"The dresses are too short," complained Rebecca.

"This is what they have," replied John. "Don't you see anything that will work?"

She selected three uniforms. John purchased two pairs of comfortable shoes and several socks to go with the uniforms. On the way back to the apartment, John stopped at a large shopping mall.

"What are we doing here?" Rebecca asked.

"You need more clothes."

"You've already spent a lot of money on me. I have everything that I need."

"Not everything," John replied. "I don't want to hear another word about how much I'm spending. As my employee, your appearance reflects on me. If you are going to work for me, you should maintain a certain appearance when you're out. Do you understand?"

"Yes, sir."

He escorted her to an upscale department store. He told a female salesclerk that he planned to purchase three outfits for Rebecca, and to include several of everything that went under them. He sat in a chair and observed the two women. Rebecca commented on the attractiveness of a blue flare midi dress with short tulip-sleeves and a tie on the left side, but refused when she saw the price tag. John cleared his throat, catching the attention of them both. He nodded in the affirmative. The next selection was white with a yellow floral wrap dress, with a V-neck and slightly bloused short sleeves. The length was higher in the front. The third was a sleeveless floral flare that rested two inches above the knees. Rebecca's face told him everything.

"Will there be shoes?" asked the clerk.

Another nod from John, set the search in motion. Rebecca settled for a black pair with two-inch block heels. The shoes were placed in a bag, and the dresses in a zipped hanging bag. John called the saleswoman over to his chair and whispered in the woman's ear.

"I understand, Mr. Walker," she replied.

She gathered a collection of feminine hygiene items and placed them in a bag. Then she escorted Rebecca to a fitting room. They remained there for more than a half hour. When the two returned to the sales floor, Rebecca avoided eye contact with John. He pretended not to notice.

When the salesperson showed her a bra, Rebecca seemed confused. The woman told her that she wore a similar garment. They left the store with the three dresses, a new slip, and an assortment of bras and panties. Rebecca had refused to wear anything with a French cut and insisted that the panties be made of cotton. In the car, John attempted in vain to strike up a conversation about the outing. She was silent until they were at the apartment.

"You're not my husband," she said.

"Of course," replied John. "I'm your employer, and I have requirements of those I hire."

"I bet you don't purchase some of these items for all your female employees!" she angrily shouted.

"True."

"You don't own me! I'm not your slave! I'll work for you, but I'm not whatever you want me to be! I decided not to cause a scene in that store, but if you ever humiliate me like that again – I promise that you will never see me again! Papers, or no stinking papers! Do you understand me?"

Her eyes were filled with a mix of rage and hurt.

"Loud and clear," John replied. "It will never happen again. I apologize for any embarrassment that I caused you."

"You marched me into that store. That woman thought I was retarded, or something. What did you say to her?"

"I just told her that you might need help with some things…I honestly tried to help you."

"No, you were dressing up your new pet, to parade around! I have a good mind to set fire to the entire lot of clothes and such."

"They are yours, to do whatever you wish. I didn't mean to…."

Rebecca loaded up her arms with everything purchased at both stores and stormed out of the room and into the spare bedroom. She loudly slammed the door.

John had not felt weariness like this since he had miserably failed his father's expectations as a teen. His eyes stared out the window, onto the vehicles and people below. His mind picked up none of it. Instead, it raced from scenario to scenario. He was wealthy. Money meant power, and he had learned how to harness it – with both men and women. This was different. There was a different side of this shy woman. Rebecca's respect for him had a limit, and John had stumbled onto it. He slumped into a chair, exhausted.

I crossed the line.

A couple of hours passed. The sun also passed

below the horizon. He stood to his feet in the darkness and turned on a couple of lamps. John had never felt so alone in his luxurious apartment. He tucked his shirt into his pants, and then moved to her bedroom door. John stood there for a moment, before giving it a knock.

"Are you hungry?" he asked. "Would you like to have dinner?"

He heard nothing. Seconds passed before the door opened. She was wearing the blue dress and the black shoes.

"Am I forgiven?" he asked. "I am truly sorry."

"I guess so," she replied.

"I'm really glad that you didn't burn the dresses."

"Is that so?"

"For two reasons. One, you look really nice in the dress."

"The other reason?' Rebecca asked.

"The smoke would have activated a sprinkler system, which disperses water from the ceiling. We both would have experienced an unintended shower."

Rebecca smiled.

66

Chapter 9
Questions

"We have a problem," said Attorney Mark Fairchild on a call to John. "We must obtain a Letter of No Record from the Georgia state registrar."

"How hard can that be?" asked John.

"We have Rebecca's name and date of birth, but we haven't conducted an exhaustive search for her birth records. I've begun that process, but it could take some time."

"What happened with the FBI and mental institution database search?" asked John. "Surely, that search could help."

"That information will be included, but we have to conduct searches for her birth from Georgia hospitals. Since she appeared near the South Carolina border, I'll need to search those hospitals also. We need evidence of a serious attempt to find birth records."

"I'll send you an advance," said John. "Call in legal assistants needing extra work. Keep me in the loop and let me know of needed resources and finances."

"This is going to cost you. Are you really sure you want to do this?"

"Absolutely."

"If we convince the state of Georgia that we have done due diligence in searching for her paperwork, then the registrar will issue a Letter of No Record to go with your letter and the affidavit."

John placed a call to the county probate office. For a charge, the county could provide records for property owners under the name Johnson going back one hundred and fifty years. He wrote a letter detailing his request and mailed it with a check. Returning from the mailbox, he found Rebecca standing in the main room.

"When I was in your Atlanta apartment, I saw a couple of interesting objects," she said.

"What objects?"

"Both the main room and your bedroom contained black rectangular objects. What were they?"

"Those are called TVs, or televisions," John replied. "They have the ability to display things. Have you ever seen a movie?"

"I've seen motion pictures," she answered. "So, these things display people moving about?"

"Let me show you," answered John, as he opened cabinet doors mounted above the fireplace.

"That's what I saw in your apartment," Rebecca said.

"Have a seat," John instructed.

She sat in her familiar chair, while John retrieved a remote control from the drawer of a lampstand beside the couch. Pressing a button, caused the equipment to come to life.

"This is a news station," explained John. "You may find it a bit boring."

"The colors and sounds are amazing," she observed, before the scene shifted to a commercial. "How does it work?"

"There's no cable service here, so I use a dish."

She stared at him in silence, as though he was speaking in a foreign language.

"Would you like to see something else?" John asked.

"I'm not sure."

"What kind of stories do you like to read?"

"I enjoyed reading a romantic story about a man and woman who met after the Great War."

"Great War, interesting term. You must be a history buff; most call it World War I. I think I may be able to find something."

John pressed buttons which caused the screen to display a menu which allowed him to conduct a search.

"You may like this one," he said. "It's called, *The Englishman Who Went Up a Hill, and Came Down a Mountain.*"

"That's a long title," she replied, with a chuckle.

"Let's give it try."

Midway through the movie, John found her wiping tears from her face. Afterwards, her eyes were still wet with tears. Rebecca gently placed her right hand on his.

"That was truly enchanting," she said.

She excused herself and made her way to her bedroom. John stepped near the door and heard weeping. An hour later, she exited the room. Her eyes were swollen.

"Would you like to watch something else on TV?" John asked.

"No," she answered. "It's a remarkable thing, like some of your other gadgets. But, I'm not ready to see any more of what it has."

As she prepared supper, she asked John to explain the importance of acquiring identification papers.

"I just don't understand why people are required to have all these papers," she said. "Is there no one who works without them?"

"There are people who work illegally without them. Those are usually people who have entered the United States illegally."

"I didn't come here illegally. I'm a US citizen. Why can't I just work those jobs?"

"Those people have to hide their identities, and they have to work for people who don't require them to produce papers. In exchange, those workers are paid very little. They are paid in secret, because if found out both the workers and the employers could be arrested."

"It sounds like a difficult life," Rebecca observed.

"If you can obtain papers, you'll be spared that life."

"Thank you. You're a decent man. I'm so fortunate to have found you."

———•●•———

Two months later, John received a package from the county deeds and records office. These records showed the history of ownership of John's property by the stream going back to 1870. John had purchased the land from Allen Alderman. The records showed that the land had been passed down to several members of the Alderman family, after it had been purchased from a Grady Johnson in 1934.

This Grady Johnson must have been an ancestor of Rebecca's husband. It's likely the name Grady had been passed down to him. It supports Rebecca's claim that the property once belonged to members of her family. This is fascinating!

John's first impulse was to share the news with Rebecca, but he decided to first obtain more information about the man.

The following week, John visited the library of the town designated as the county seat. He researched census records stored on micro-fiche, since lack of government funding had prevented the effort to digitalize the information for Web use. The 1930 census showed Grady Johnson as age thirty-six and living alone, but the 1920 census showed him to be married to a woman named Rebecca. John paid the small fee to have the information printed on hard copy. As he waited for the copies, he thought about how he would share his findings with the woman living in his cabin.

Rebecca should be relieved to know that I found evidence to support her story. This county has a very small population. What are the chances of two couples named Grady and Rebecca Johnson being somewhat associated with my property?

Suddenly, a cold shiver hit John squarely at the base of his neck.

Is it possible that Rebecca is familiar with the account of this couple living in the county one hundred years before? Oh, God! Did she take on the story of these people as her own experience?

Chapter 10
Confrontation

"I want to know about that cult in the woods," John demanded after returning from the county seat.

"I can't tell you anything about that," Rebecca replied.

"You signed a statement certifying that you were raised in a cult that separated you from society. I want to know the details."

"That cult was your idea, not mine," she replied.

"What? Are you telling me that you lied? You said that it was true."

"If you'll remember, you asked me if I had a better explanation of my lack of paperwork than that cult story. I told you that I didn't. I don't have a better explanation, but I don't know anything about a cult."

"Mark was right about you! I should have listened. You've been playing me the whole time. I can't believe it!"

"You're the one who told me that I had to have papers, and that I had no other option than to sign that letter," she shot back.

"Now, I know that you made up the entire story about marrying a man named Grady Johnson," John stated, handing her the printouts from the library.

"I don't know what this is, but my husband's name was Grady Johnson."

"Stop it! Who are you?"

"Rebecca Johnson," she said, tossing the papers on the kitchen table.

"No, Rebecca Johnson was married to a Grady Johnson a hundred years ago. I'll have to hand it to you. You're incredibly smart and you're a gifted liar.'

Rebecca slapped John hard across his face and bolted from the cabin. He chased after her.

"You can't just run from this!" he yelled. "We're both in a mess now. We're joined at the hip on this thing. You and I have falsified documents sent to the US government. This is serious."

"I've had enough of this," she replied. "I can't stay here another minute."

"Don't you understand what will happen to me and my business, if the government finds out we lied on those documents?"

"You told me that I had no other option, so I signed them. Now you're calling me a liar, and I won't stand for it."

"What do you call signing your name on false statements?" John asked. "We both signed, and that makes us both liars. The difference is that I thought you were telling me the truth. I believed you."

"I didn't lie to you."

"When are you going to tell me the truth?" John demanded.

"You wouldn't believe the truth, and I wouldn't believe someone if they told me the truth about all of this."

"Try me," said John.

"Listen, the only real lie was the signing of that document, and I was made to feel that I had to do that. I'm not a liar."

"OK, so tell me what really happened."

"I'm really sorry that you were pulled into all of this. I'm sorry about the signed documents."

Rebecca turned and walked up the drive toward the road. John rushed to her side, and gently took her by the arm.

"Please don't leave," he said. "We have to sort this out."

"You said that there are those who find work without papers, and that's what I need to do. You need to let me go."

"This is nuts! What do you plan to do?"

"I'll hitch a ride to Atlanta. Out of a place that large, I should be able to find the kind of work that you talked about."

"Some of the women entering the country illegally are forced into prostitution," explained John. "You shouldn't get mixed up with these people."

"You should …"

John pulled her close to him.

"Please stay," he said. "Come back inside."

"It's not really fair to you."

"If something terrible happened to you by hooking up with those people, I'm not sure that I could handle it."

Without saying another word, he took her by the

hand and led her back inside the cabin.

"Have a seat at the kitchen table, and I'll put coffee on," John told her.

"Where did you find this information?" she asked, while looking over the copies on the table.

"At a library. It had census records going back to 1870."

Rebecca silently reviewed the records. Within minutes, John placed two cups of coffee on the table.

"We need to make some decisions," he began.

"Are you going to tell your lawyer that we falsely signed those documents?" Rebecca asked.

"I think it might be too late to undo all of that."

"I can't tell you the truth, but I promise that I won't lie to you," Rebecca pledged.

"You promise…"

"Do you have a Bible around?"

"There is one in the drawer of a lamp stand in the next room," said John. "It was given to me by a couple of people who came by. They invited me to their church."

"Please get it."

John retrieved the Bible and placed it in front of Rebecca. She stood and placed her left hand on the Bible. With the open palm of her right hand held near her face, she spoke.

"I swear that my name is Rebecca Johnson, and that I will never lie to John Walker, so help me God."

"Well…"

"I rarely swear oaths, and you saw me put my hand on the Bible," she said.

"That, I did," replied John.

"Then, it's settled. You can rest in the fact that I

won't lie to you."

Her oath didn't provide rest to John's mind.

I've falsified documents and I honestly don't know what to do. I've blindly placed my cards on the table. It may make matters worse to try put them back in my hand. I want to call Mark, but I'm afraid there's no turning back.

———•●•———

Three weeks later, John received the call he had awaited from his attorney.

"We have the Letter of No Record from both Georgia and South Carolina, and I'm submitting the paperwork today."

"Thanks, Mark," replied John.

"I'm sending the paperwork required for Rebecca Johnson to be issued a Social Security Number. You're almost done with this little project of yours, but you may not like my bill for the effort."

"I'll be glad to pay it. You have no idea what a relief it will be."

78

Chapter 11
Photo

Though the conflict between John and Rebecca had been settled by her obtaining a Social Security Number, his curiosity about her continued. There were too many unanswered questions. John flipped through library micro-fiche containing photos of county events during 1920. The census records of that year showed Grady and Rebecca Johnson as a married couple, and he was driven to find out all he could about them.

I still believe Rebecca has falsely patterned stories about her life, based on this couple from the past. If I find out more about these people, I may be able to separate fact from fiction.

He came across a photo of local area World War I veterans and their wives. The names of the men were printed below the picture.

Grady Johnson! At last, a face to go with the name. Oh, my God!

There, standing next to the man identified in the

photo as Grady Johnson, was a woman who struck an incredible likeness to Rebecca. He had two printed copies made.

Arriving back at the cabin, he found Rebecca busily vacuuming. John placed one photo in the safe in his bedroom closet, and he brought the other into the main room.

"How was your morning?" asked Rebecca, as she unplugged the vacuum.

"Interesting," John replied. "I'd like to show you a photo. Come, I'll place it on the kitchen table."

Rebecca dutifully put the vacuum away and sat at the table near John.

"Take a look at this," he said.

Rebecca's face looked as if she had seen a ghost. She held the photo in her right hand, her left held over her mouth.

"This is a photo of…"

"Grady," interrupted Rebecca. "Were did you get this?"

"The county library is small, but it's amazing what can be found there," answered John.

"This was right after the war, in 1920. I remem…"

Rebecca stopped in mid-sentence. Shaking hands placed the photo back on the table. Haunting eyes met Johns.

"What were you about to say?" he asked.

"Nothing."

"You've seen this photo before, haven't you?" pressed John.

Rebecca nodded.

"It was this photo that gave you the idea of

pretending to be Rebecca, married to a man named Grady Johnson," accused John.

"No."

She slowly rose from the table, collected her recently purchased purse, and made her way to the front door of the cabin.

"You've been very kind to me," she said.

With those few words, she slipped out of the door. A setting sun peeked between large trees surrounding the cabin. Several minutes passed, before John decided to go after her in his SUV. Just as he found her months before, she was at the small tombstone of Lilly Johnson in the cemetery beside St. Paul's Methodist Church.

"What are you doing?" asked John.

"I think it's time for me to leave your cabin and find a place of my own," she answered. "I have the paperwork required for employment now, so I shouldn't impose on your hospitality any longer."

"There's no rush for you to leave."

"I think there is. I've been with you long enough."

"What brought this on?"

"I know now that I'm not trusted, and that there's really no way of gaining that trust. I appreciate the generosity you've shown me. I have the required papers, and I've saved a little over one hundred dollars. I plan to move to move to Atlanta and find work."

"That's not enough to even pay the deposit on a place to rent," John explained.

"I hate being here!" she shouted. "I should be buried here, right beside…"

Tears of frustration and sadness poured down her face. She turned to walk away, but John prevented her retreat by stepping in front of her. Her shoulders slumped in brokenness; she wept. John pulled her close, and she melted into his chest.

"You shouldn't be buried anywhere, and I don't want to hear you say things like that," he said. "It's obvious that you carry secrets that are like lead weights, and it's apparent that you don't trust me enough to share them."

"I can't explain some things. There's simply no way to tell anyone. I've tried, but I don't belong in this world."

"Sure, you do. What do you think of the chances that you would find someone like me, with means to help you establish citizenship and provide you with a comfortable life? Whether it was God or fate, I believe I was supposed to help you. Think about it."

"I really don't know what to think about anything. I've lost my husband and a daughter, and I've been pushed into a strange world. I've lost everything that mattered to me. You talk about God. Why would God do that to me? What did I do? Why did this happen?"

"I can't answer those questions," John replied. "I know little of your past because you refuse to trust me with it. I know that none of us can change the past, and that the future isn't guaranteed. What you have is the present, and that's all anyone has. I believe that I'm supposed to help you with the present. Try to rest in that."

Still holding Rebecca, he felt her take a deep breath.

"You don't deserve secrecy, and you don't deserve to be stuck with me," Rebecca whispered.

"And you've stated that you don't believe you

should have suffered those losses," John added. "For now, how about we let go of the past. I'll help you get your present life rolling. Atlanta's a big place, and there are certainly a number of work opportunities. What kind of work do you want?"

"All I seem to be able to do is clean."

"I think you have more potential, but we can begin with that. I'll make a few calls."

John led her to his SUV and brought her back to the cabin. He suggested that she rest in the bedroom while he considered options for Rebecca. Taking a seat at the kitchen table, John powered up his laptop. While waiting for a connection through his Wi-Fi, he glanced over at the photo of Grady Johnson and his wife. John considered the fact that Rebecca's husband could have been named after a great grandfather. His focus was on the woman in the photo.

That man's wife could pass for Rebecca's twin. I've heard of inter-family marriages in the Georgia mountains. It's possible the woman could be both Rebecca's and her husband's great grandmother. Who knows?

84

Chapter 12
The Article

"**Anybody around?**" **John** called out, as he cautiously opened the front door of his Atlanta condo.

"Just me," answered Rebecca. "I thought you might go to the cabin as soon as you got back in town."

"I did, but the place just seemed empty. Plus, I have a meeting here tomorrow. How's the job?"

"I was given a raise last week."

"Great!" John exclaimed, while dropping a couple of travel bags on the floor, and then taking a seat in his favorite chair. "I knew you would excel."

"I would have never found the job at that fancy hotel on my own. Everyone there is jealous of the fact that you allow me to live in this apartment."

"Jealous? Do they know that you come back here and clean the place?"

"If I save a little more, I should be able to move out on my own. You've been more than gracious, but I should go."

"You seem to always want to be going

somewhere. Just relax. You can't afford anything in this neighborhood, and you don't have a car."

"It just isn't right."

"What's not right?" asked John.

"People think things."

"What things?"

"They think that you're my daddy. I can't seem to convince them otherwise."

"I'm not that much older than you, twelve years."

"No, they think that I'm your woman."

"I've found that people believe what they want to believe. You can't help what people think."

"I'm not a quiff. I was once a married woman."

"Where did you come up with quiff?" asked John. "You grew up with several interesting words."

"It simply means that I'm not a loose woman."

"You certainly aren't" agreed John. "Did you try out that church?"

"I don't seem to fit there. The people either have money, or they want to hob-nob with people who do. I work at a hotel."

"That's too bad."

"Enough about me. How was Europe?" prodded Rebecca.

"Interesting. A lot of very old buildings, and a lot of foreign languages."

"When did you get back?"

"A week ago. I told you that I was at the cabin. I found something that puzzles me."

"What?"

John motioned for her to take a seat across from him on the couch. He pulled a sheet of paper from his jacket, unfolded it, and handed the copy of an old newspaper article to her.

"What's this?" she asked.

"Just read it."

After scanning the words, she closed her eyes and held the copy to her breasts with both hands. Her lips quivered. John studied every feature of her troubled face.

"Why would Grady Johnson's wife just disappear like that?" asked John.

"I can't imagine how he felt," she answered. "I've been so focused on my own situation, I never once considered what Grady faced."

"This article was written in 1934. I found it on micro-fiche at that county library, while researching information about the property that I own. Why does a situation someone faced ninety years ago bother you?"

Her eyes glanced about the room.

"I've been helping you out for six months," stated John. "Haven't I earned your trust by now? Don't you think it's time you leveled with me?"

Rebecca sat in silence. Avoiding John, her eyes again focused on the article.

"What are your thoughts about this article?" asked John. "I think you know more about this than you let on."

Placing the article on the arm of the couch, she nervously rubbed her hands.

"Why did Grady's wife leave him, never to return?" demanded John. "I think you know something, because I believe this man was your Grady's great grandfather."

"You know what they say about making assumptions," she replied.

"I've heard the phrase. Stop avoiding my questions."

"Why are so obsessed with this?" she asked.

"What do you know about why this woman left her husband?" John pressed. "Did the men in your husband's family have issues with anger? Was this man abusive? Did he beat her?"

"Never!" Rebecca shouted. "He never hit me...not even once."

"Hit you?" asked John.

"Aggghh! Why can't you leave this alone?"

Rebecca shot up out of her seat on the couch and paced around the room. Her eyes were wild. Her hands shook.

"Talk to me," John commanded. "I believe you've seen this article before, and it provided you with ideas."

"Just stop!"

She was like a caged animal. The pacing hastened. Her eyes were frantic.

"Relax," encouraged John. "You look like you're about to explode. Can't you just talk to me? Why did seeing this article trigger this reaction in you?"

"Please stop," she begged.

"What's going on with you?"

Rebecca grabbed her coat and headed for the door. John launched himself from the chair and cut her off.

"Don't run away," he said. "Every time I try to get you to open up, you take off."

"Get out of my way!"

"Not this time," John insisted.

"Please."

"Tell me why you're so upset," John requested.

"You'll think…you'll think that I'm either goofy or zozzled."

"Zozzled? What's with these words of yours?"

She turned her back on him, and nervously took a few steps. John silently waited, while she attempted to compose herself. Suddenly, she turned and approached him. He could tell that beneath her calm demeanor, her emotions could easily erupt.

"Why can't you leave the past alone?" Rebecca asked. "Talking about it won't help anything."

"I want you to be honest with me."

"I wouldn't expect you to believe me, if I was honest with you. I wouldn't believe it, if someone told me. Please, leave me alone."

"I don't want to leave you alone," John said.

"Please."

"I'm not going to leave you alone, and that includes your past. I know that you're dealing with something that is taking its toll on you. At least tell me why this article has upset you."

"It's my burden to bear, and I can't talk about it."

"Cut that out!" John blurted. "Why are you so bothered by the fact that Grady's wife, Rebecca, ran out on him?"

"Because I'm that Rebecca!" she shouted.

Her knees buckled, and she dropped to the floor.

Chapter 13
Explanation

"**Are you all** right?" John asked, kneeling beside Rebecca.

"No," she answered. "The entire world has been a nightmare for months. I'm definitely not all right."

John sat down beside her.

"Talk to me," he said.

"When I walked out of those woods, when you first met me, I was stepping out of the year 1922," Rebecca said.

"What?"

"There. I told you. You can do whatever. You can put me in the looney bin or kick me out. I really don't care anymore. Maybe I need to be put in a looney bin."

"You believe that you jumped from 1922 to the present?"

"I don't believe it; I know it," she replied. "One minute I was walking down to the stream to relax after washing dishes, and the next minute I was telling you not to fish on our property. I was angry with you, until you showed me your cabin. That threw me for a loop. I was in shock. I raced back to my home, only to find it in ruins. I remember glancing down at myself. My clothes were the same, but everything else had changed."

"How could that happen?" John questioned.

"How would I know?" Rebecca shouted.

"I'm not sure what to do with that."

"You think that YOU'RE not sure! What do you think I've been going through? I told you that you wouldn't believe me."

"You're saying that you were the woman standing with Grady Johnson in the photo of World War I vets?" asked John.

"You keep calling it World War, but it was the Great War. It was the war to end all wars. Grady had nightmares. He would wake up shaking. About a year after he got back from the front, he began telling me about some of his experiences. It was horrible."

"It certainly didn't end all wars," John said. "This story of yours about time travel is pretty weird. Have you felt that something like this has happened to you before?"

"Of course not. I'm not a rubber ball bouncing around history. I knew that you would think that I'm batty. I didn't want to talk about it. Why did you have to keep pressuring me about things?"

"You have a tendency to run away, each time I confront you. I remember when you ran off to that church cemetery."

"My daughter's grave," said Rebecca. "It was the only thing that remained the same. Lily's grave let me know that I wasn't completely crazy. But when I took a look at the graves around hers, the dates made no sense."

"Was that why you were crying when I found you there?" asked John.

"I'm usually sad when I visit her grave, but this time it was different. Its presence grounded me, until I saw other tombstones. Once it dawned on me that the dates on the other graves were real, I realized what had happened to me. I began to understand why my house was gone. Those dates also told me that Grady couldn't still be alive. It was further confirmed when I saw the date on the newspaper at Sally's Café. I'll never see him again. I can't imagine how he felt about my disappearance. He suffered so much in the war. It isn't fair."

"I'm not saying that I buy into all the time travel stuff, but I can see how believing that would certainly be upsetting."

"I've lost everything," said Rebecca. "I lost my daughter, my husband, and my home. I've lost my entire world. I don't belong here."

"Maybe you were right. Maybe it's best that you focus on the present."

"Why has God been punishing me? I wondered if my daughter's death was punishment, but now this has happened. I don't know what I've done to turn God against me."

"I can't speak for God," John said. "I'm not even sure that God exists. You think that God made you travel through time? But is something like that even in the Bible?"

"I don't know of time travel happening in the Bible, but it talks about God moving people from place to place."

"You mean like teleporting somebody around?" asked John.

"I don't know what teleporting is, but the Bible says that God suddenly moved Phillip from one place to another."

"Where does it say that?"

"I can't remember," answered Rebecca. "Perhaps, if we found a Bible."

"I have the internet on my cell phone. I can just look it up."

"You have what?" asked Rebecca.

John quickly typed into the internet search application on his cell, "God moving Philip."

"Acts 8:39," John said.

"That thing can tell you about Bible verses?" asked Rebecca.

"You can find a lot of things with this," answered John. "It says that the Spirit of God suddenly took Phillip away, and that the Ethiopian eunuch never saw Philip again."

"That's the Bible story."

"Well, if God is the master of space, God could also be the master of time."

"I thought you didn't believe in God," said Rebecca, taking a seat in a chair.

"I'm not saying that I believe in God. I'm just saying that if a being was the master of space in this manner, it would also master time. That's all."

"God's a He, not an it," said Rebecca.

"I wouldn't know. If you say so, I'm not going to argue. To instantaneously move someone from one place to another, involves both space and time. I'm just following the logic. Do you believe that God instantaneously moved Philip from one place to another?"

"Yes, I don't question the Bible," Rebecca replied.

"Then a god like this can just as easily move someone through time," said John. "The fourth dimension is time. A minute ago, you weren't in that chair. Now, you are. However, it took time for you to move to it. An instantaneous move into that chair might require the temporary absence of time. So, it would require the mastery of both space and time."

"So, you believe God moved me through time in the blink of an eye?"

"I'm not saying that I believe what you told me, I'm just saying that your Bible story is consistent with it."

"I can't explain it, but you've made me feel better."

As John took a seat on the couch across from Rebecca, his mind was unsettled.

I'm not feeling better about this situation. I wonder if she really believes this crap about time travel, or if this is simply just an attempt to manipulate me. In either case, I'd best be careful.

96

Chapter 14
The Gift

"What are your plans for the future?" John asked Rebecca. "I believe you have more potential than cleaning rooms at a hotel."

"It's honest work, and I seem to be appreciated by the hotel management," she replied.

"I have something that I want to show you," John said, pulling a brochure from his coat. "I'd like for you to read this and consider what's offered."

"What is this?"

"It's a list of two-year degrees and certificates offered by a local community college. There is a short description of each. The courses are offered online, and I'm willing to pay for your tuition and books. You would be able to take these classes after getting off work."

"I appreciate your willingness to pay for this, but I think you're doing more than enough for me already. You found me a job, and you're allowing me to live here rent free. This place is the cat's meow. Besides, I don't think that I'm cut out for college."

"These courses could open new opportunities for you. Will you look this over, give it serious consideration? See if anything looks interesting"

"I will. Thank you."

"I have something else for you," John said, while unzipping a travel bag. "I bought you a laptop."

"That's too much! You shouldn't spend that kind of money on me."

"Hold on. This isn't just for you. I was troubled to find that I had difficulties reaching you while I was in Europe."

"You called the man at the desk several times, and he was kind enough to provide the messages to me. Did he not contact you with my reply?"

"He did, but I really shouldn't have troubled him. I want to be able to reach you more often when I'm away and reach you directly. This would help solve the problem. Come over to the kitchen table, and I'll show you a few things."

"I'm afraid that I would break it."

"Don't worry. Please, sit down. I've already set up a personal account for you. Watch what I do. There are two main things that you have to remember. Your username is *Rebecca1922* and your password is *GradyJohnson*. You should be able to easily remember both."

"So, you do believe me. I'm glad. It's such a relief to be honest with you about what happened to me."

"Why don't we stick to the subject at hand?" John suggested, avoiding her comment. "There are several things that I would like to show you."

Rebecca wasn't deterred.

"What did your lawyer say when you told him?"

she asked.

"Told him what?"

"What did he say when you told him the truth about me jumping from the year 1922?"

"Our conversations have been focused on my business. That's why I have him on retainer. Now, I want to show you how to use the laptop. Pay close attention."

John showed her how to log in and explained the concept of email. He even sent a test email from the laptop's email application to his personal email address, and then replied using his cell phone. He had her use the laptop to reply back to him, and he showed her how it arrived instantaneously on his cell.

"That's amazingly fast!" Rebecca observed.

"If I travel to Europe again, we would be able to converse easily using email," John said.

"How long does it take this kind of mail to reach another machine across the seas?" Rebecca asked.

"Seconds. It really depends on the particular machine and rate of speed of the internet provider."

"How is it possible for censors to read that kind of mail in just seconds?" Rebecca questioned.

"Censors?"

"When Grady was in the war, it took days for mail to reach me. The Red Cross collected the mail and took the letters to military censors. If there was no questionable information contained in the letter, it was released to be sent to me in the states."

"There are no censors, the information travels by satellites and by cables. No one reads the information before it reaches a destination."

"I understand cables. It must be a sort of telegraph

system. What are sat…what did you call them?"

"Satellites are machines circling the earth in space. Information is relayed from the earth, up to a satellite, and then relayed back down to a different place on earth. It's very fast."

"Circling the earth?"

Rebecca stood. Obvious disappointment was on her face. She slowly made her way to her bedroom, entered and closed the door. Bewildered, John followed. He gingerly knocked on the door.

"Yes?" she softly spoke.

"Can I come in?"

"Yes."

"What's going on with you? Did I upset you somehow?"

"I've opened myself up to you," she explained. "I've been completely honest with you about what really happened to me. I'd hoped that, in return, you would be honest with me."

"I'm absolutely being honest with you."

"You talked about machines that are in space, circling the earth like the moon, and relaying messages to individual people on the earth. Next, will you try to tell me that people have been walking around on the moon?"

"Let me show you something else," offered John, ignoring her question.

Her arms crossed in silence; she glared at him. John exited the room, retrieved the laptop, sat down on the bed beside her, and placed the laptop on his lap.

"Do you want to see what I meant by satellites?" he asked.

She watched him type into the internet browser,

satellites in space. He selected an article which showed pictures of several satellites and text regarding each.

"This is what I was talking about," he explained. "You see, I was telling you the truth. With this search engine, you can quickly find information about a host of subjects."

"Can we search for something else?" she asked.

"Sure."

"Look up four-ninety truck," she said. "Put a dash between the words four and ninety."

John keyed it into the browser, and a photo of a 1918 Chevrolet Four-Ninety truck was displayed. She starred at it in disbelief. Rebecca's wide eyes met John's.

"Grady wanted one of those so bad he could taste it," she said. "This machine of yours is almost frightening."

"This is yours. It's a gift. You can ask it anything you wish, by just typing on this search field."

"Can it find a song?"

"We can try."

"Find *Make Believe*, by Nora Bayes," Rebecca said.

John keyed in her request, and a recording was displayed. He selected it, and music played over the laptop. At first, Rebecca smiled. Then her head dropped.

"Please turn it off," she softly requested.

John could tell that she was genuinely disturbed.

"That song means something to you, doesn't it?" he asked.

She lifted her head. Tear-filled eyes provided the answer.

102

Chapter 15
Make Believe

WHAT WAS THE NAME OF THAT SONG?
John remembered.
Make Believe. That's what she wanted to hear.
He looked up the lyrics,

There are times when you feel sad and blue
Something's wrong, you don't know what to do
When you feel that way, stop and think awhile
Just make believe and smile

Make believe you are glad when you're sorry
Sunshine will follow the rain
When things go wrong, it won't be long
Soon they'll be right again

Tho' your love dreams have gone, make believe,
don't let on
Smile tho' your heart may be broken
For when bad luck departs, you will find good
luck starts

Don't grieve, just make believe

When your dearest friends have turned away
And blue skies above have turned to gray
Don't worry for it may not all be true
Here's my advice to you

Make believe you are glad when you're sorry
Sunshine will follow the rain
When things go wrong, it won't be long
Soon they'll be right again

Tho' your love dreams have gone, make believe,
don't let on
Smile tho' your heart may be broken
For when bad luck departs, you will find good
luck starts
Don't grieve, just make believe

John mumbled to himself.
Is that what's she doing? Is she pretending?

— • ● • —

John found Rebecca at the kitchen table busily typing on the keyboard of the laptop he had given her.

"Hello," he greeted.

"Hello," she returned, not looking up.

"I see that you've lost your apprehension about the laptop."

"This thing is fascinating," she said, still typing. "Do people still go to libraries?"

John chuckled.

"People go to libraries to research particular subjects," he answered. "The problem with articles found on the internet, is that some may not be completely true."

"What?" she blurted, now looking up.

"Most articles from professional sites can be trusted, but there are articles posted by people who aren't very knowledgeable. Then there are weird groups which post lies."

"How can this be trusted?" she asked.

"It's best to learn which sites are factual, and it's also a good idea to read a number of articles about a particular subject."

"I see. So, it's like talking to people. Someone may be spreading gossip, so it's best to ask more than one person."

"Exactly," John replied. "What have you found that interests you?"

"I found that people have been to the moon," she replied. "I found that you were right about the Great War. It certainly didn't end all wars, and that the next war ended with the use of an unimaginably terrible weapon. I would have never imagined."

"It was unfortunate that the Japanese government refused to surrender before those weapons were used. However, there are estimates that the use of those two nuclear weapons probably saved hundreds of thousands of Allied and Japanese lives, possibly millions. The Japanese refused to surrender, even after the use of the first bomb."

"I could have never imagined a weapon so terrible."

"Hopefully, those weapons will never be used

again."

John excused himself to change clothes. After a few minutes, he heard Rebecca cry out.

"Oh, my word! How do I turn this off?"

As he left his bedroom, he saw her slam the laptop closed.

"What's going on?" John asked.

"I can't believe someone would broadcast that!" she shouted.

"What did you see?" he asked, opening the laptop.

There on the screen was a clip from a pornographic movie.

"I see," said John, hitting the escape button.

"Why would a woman allow herself to be filmed like this?" she asked.

"Why have some women prostituted themselves since the beginning of time?" he asked, with a wink. "I think this is simply a continuation of things which have been going for a very long time."

"I guess you're right. I wasn't searching for that. Why was this shown?"

"I'm guessing that you unknowingly selected a link to that site."

Rebecca again closed the laptop and pushed it away.

"I forgot to install the virus scanning software. I'll do that. Also, there are internet settings that can disable the display of some of that kind of information."

"Information? You call that information?"

"I'll install a virus scanning application. Would you want me to limit the search capability?"

"I don't need to see that," she replied.

"You were married, correct?"

"Yes."

"Then, I would guess that you've witnessed that before."

"That's supposed to be private; not shared with the world," she said, giving John a stern look.

"I suppose you're right."

"That man was huge," Rebecca remarked.

John grinned. Rebecca rolled her eyes.

"How long did you watch before closing the lid?" he asked.

"Not very long!" she shouted

John couldn't contain his laughter any longer.

"Men," she said, with a slight twinkle in her eyes.

John had witnessed a different side of Rebecca.

So, that strait-laced behavior of hers has been partially an act. That's interesting. I should have known.

Chapter 16
DNA

"**There has been** a development," began attorney Mark Fairchild, on a call to John. "A hunter has found two badly decomposed bodies in the northeast Georgia mountains. They were under a deteriorating collapsed teepee."

"Do you believe these people were members of the cult Bobby Thompson told me about?" asked John.

"The FBI was called in because the bodies were found near the North Carolina state line."

"The FBI? Is foul play suspected?"

"I wasn't given those details," answered the attorney. "I was told that they are trying to determine the identity of the two. I was contacted because I represented Rebecca Johnson in establishing her citizenship. Her documented account of living with a cult in those mountains caused her case to be flagged. They want to sample her DNA for a possible match to these bodies."

"What does this involve?"

"An autosomal DNA test is done by a swab of the inside her cheek. They plan to come by your apartment tomorrow afternoon."

"She'll still be at work," explained John.

"Would she rather the FBI come to her workplace?"

"I see your point. I'll talk to her and her employer."

"If they find a match, it would certainly validate her account of why she didn't have documented citizenship," said Fairchild.

John's mind raced as the call ended.

Rebecca indicated that the cult story was of my making. That, and her current claims of time travel, seem to be a desperate effort to avoid telling the truth about her past. I'm interested in seeing her reaction when told that she is under the microscope of the FBI.

— • ● • —

"You seem nervous," remarked John. "You've been pacing the room for the past ten minutes."

"You told me that FBI agents are going to run a test to determine if I'm related to dead people," replied Rebecca. "Wouldn't that make you feel odd?"

"Possibly. In my case, a relationship with them would be doubtful."

A knock on the door of the apartment interrupted the conversation. Rebecca grabbed John's right arm with both hands. He placed his left hand on one of hers, and she quickly composed herself. Her hands left John's arm, and she straightened her dress just before the door was opened. Both agents flashed badges identifying themselves. John promptly ushered them into the main room.

"Mr. Walker," stated agent Jefferson.

"Yes."

"I understand that you are Rebecca Johnson?" asked agent Wilson.

"I am," she replied.

"May I see an ID?"

Rebecca quickly retrieved her Social Security card and photo ID as an employee of the hotel from her purse in the kitchen. She handed both to agent Wilson.

"Thank you," he said, handling them to Jefferson.

Rebecca watched intently as agent Jefferson snapped photos of each using a cell phone before returning them to her. Agent Wilson pulled a small kit from his jacket and showed it to her.

"Ms. Johnson, this is called a DNA test kit and the evidence that is taken today will be submitted to our DNA Support Unit," explained the agent. "The test results will be stored in the National DNA Index System. I will use four swabs to painlessly take cells from the inside of your cheek. Do you understand?"

"Yes, John explained some of this to me before you came," answered Rebecca.

"This is a form stating your voluntary participation in this investigation," agent Jefferson stated, handing her a form and a pen. "Please read and sign."

Rebecca glanced over to John, who nodded approval of the signature. She quickly signed and handed the form and pen to the agent. Agent Wilson asked her to open her mouth, and Wilson quickly swabbed the inside of both cheeks and placed each swab in separate paper envelopes.

"That's it," said the agent, placing the envelopes in his jacket.

"When should we know the results?" asked John.

"Ms. Johnson will be contacted within a couple of weeks," stated agent Wilson.

———•●•———

Ten days later, Rebecca and John were again visited by the agents. They explained that the visit would be much longer than the first, so John suggested that everyone take a seat.

"Ms. Johnson, we have the results of the DNA testing in this envelope," said agent Wilson, handing it to her. "The bodies found in the mountains were of a man and woman. You will see that the test revealed a positive match to the man, and negative to the woman. We believe the man may be your father, since the autopsy showed the individual to be between fifty and sixty. The woman was much younger."

"My father?" asked Rebecca.

"In your written statement, you said that your father had passed away," he said. "When was the last time that you saw him?"

Rebecca nervously glanced around the room, before looking at John. His face showed curiosity for the answer.

"I suppose it was about a week before I met Mr. Walker," she replied.

The agent looked at John.

"That was more than six months ago," John said.

"Was your father alive when you last saw him?"

asked agent Wilson.

"Yes," she answered.

"So, can you explain why you stated that he has passed away?" Wilson asked.

"I was told that he was no longer living," she said.

"By who?" questioned the agent.

"I don't have an answer."

"You were told by a stranger that your father was dead, and you didn't bother to find out for yourself whether this was true?" asked Wilson.

"I left the place where my father was, and I couldn't go back," she answered.

"Why not?"

"I just felt that it was impossible."

"We really need more information about this," said Wilson.

"I don't have more information to give you."

"It's important that you provide us with more information, because we are investigating two homicides," the agent explained.

"I think I should contact my attorney," interjected John.

114

Chapter 17
Desperation

"**Let's talk this** through," suggested Mark Fairchild. "It seems that the DNA results corroborate the story of Rebecca's parents living in the north Georgia mountains. So, what's the real problem?"

"The problem is that the FBI is requesting information that Rebecca is reluctant to provide," answered John.

"You've been pretty tight-lipped all along," said Mark, turning to Rebecca. "Now that the FBI is involved, you may need to be more forthcoming."

"I can't talk about some things," she replied.

"John told me that you didn't go back to see about your father after hearing that he died," said Mark. "That's understandable, if the two of you had an extremely poor relationship. Do you feel like you would dishonor your father by stating so?"

"It's more complicated than that," she answered.

"John said that someone told you that he passed away," said the attorney. "Are you trying to protect this person?"

Rebecca sat in silence, wringing her hands. Her eyes darted.

"You need to tell us the truth, so that Mark has the information he needs," coaxed John. "You need his help."

Her wide eyes locked onto John's.

"The truth is that I was born in 1896!" she blurted.

"Oh, God!" John cried out, placing both hands over his face. "You can't…"

"I can't tell him the truth?" asked Rebecca. "You told me to tell him the truth!"

"What the hell is going on?" asked Mark.

"Good grief," John said, with a sigh. "I give up."

"Rebecca, will you excuse John and me for a moment?" asked Mark.

Mark motioned for John to step outside the apartment. Once outside, he stepped directly in front of his client.

"You need to explain what just happened in there," the attorney demanded.

"A few days ago, I pressed her for the truth about the past," John replied. "She came up with a story about traveling through time."

"What?"

"She came up with a story about unwillingly passing from 1922 to the present on the day we met. I was just as shocked as you. I listened, thinking that it was just another diversion from the truth about her past."

"Please tell me that she didn't start that with the FBI."

"No, she clammed up. She told them that she

couldn't explain things. When the FBI revealed they were investigating a murder, I stopped the conversation with a statement about needing to consult with an attorney."

"You did the right thing. Is she mentally stable?"

"She seems sane. I don't know what she is hiding, and I'm as lost as you are about her claims about traveling through time. I honestly don't know why she came up with that story."

"With the DNA match, we have a solid story about the cult situation," noted Mark. "If she left that group prior to her father's death, then she simply needs a rational explanation as to why she didn't go back when she learned of it. Maybe she is afraid of another member of the cult."

"That would make perfect sense," said John.

"We need to push that line of reasoning when we go back inside."

"Agreed. I'll let you take the lead this time. When I attempted to press her, she went H.G. Wells with me. We have to make her understand that there can't be any talk of time travel with the FBI."

"Wells wrote *The Time Machine* in 1895," said Mark. "It's certainly been around long enough to be considered a classic by some. I would have no clue as to what a primitive cult would allow as reading material, but I'm guessing she's acquainted with the story."

"What can be so terrible that she goes to such lengths to avoid talking about her past?"

"Have you ever seen marks on her?"

"No, but she keeps most of her body covered. I've only seen her face, arms and lower legs."

"Most defensive marks would be on the arms, but they could have tied her down and done other things," suggested Mark.

"You're suggesting sexual abuse?"

"It wouldn't be the first time a cult participated in that behavior. She said that she lost a child, didn't she?"

"She also said that she was married to a man named Grady," said John.

"Ethically, she appears to be pretty conservative, doesn't she?"

"That's an understatement, but I get the feeling that she believes that behavior is expected of her."

"Do you think that she would openly admit to being raped?"

"I see what you're saying," said John. "No, she wouldn't."

"We've been outside your apartment for a while. She's probably wondering what we're doing."

When the two returned inside, they found Rebecca standing in the kitchen, holding a large knife above her left wrist. Her eyes were wild.

Chapter 18
A Plan

"**Please put the** knife down." John begged of Rebecca.

He approached her slowly, carefully considering his actions, should she follow through. Mark helplessly stood just inside the door of the apartment.

"Stop!" she commanded. "Don't come any closer."

"We'll figure out how to proceed," promised John, halting his progress in her direction. "Please put the knife down."

"No one seems to be able to leave me alone," she said. "You press me for information about my life, the woman at the café wanted more information. When I obtained the paperwork that everyone demands that I have, I thought all of this would stop. It didn't. Now, the FBI is demanding more from me. This is never going to stop."

"It will eventually stop," said John. "We just need to calmly discuss how to go forward."

"No, I've read Dante's *Inferno*!" she shouted. "This cycle never ends."

"It ends with the FBI. If we satisfy the FBI, where else could this go? Mark and I have been discussing a way forward. Just stop this, and let's talk it through."

"It ends with me telling them the truth, and me spending the rest of my stinking life in a nuthouse."

"We don't need to go in that direction. Just stop and listen to the two of us. You aren't alone in this. You know that. Haven't I been there for you?"

As he spoke, John continued a slow and methodical approach in her direction. Soon he was close enough to be a target of the knife.

"Please put that down," he calmly requested. "Please."

"I don't know what else I can do to make this go away," she whispered.

"I've proved that I want to take care of you, and I will continue to do so," John said. "Do you trust me?"

"I don't trust the FBI."

"Mark and I are in your corner. We are standing between you and the FBI. We have a plan. Please stop and listen."

The knife was dropped in the kitchen sink with an almost deafening sound. Rebecca's body was shaking. John quickly moved to take her in his arms. She wept aloud. A minute later, he felt the rigid tension leave her body. He slowly reached for a box of tissues on the counter and brought it before her swollen eyes.

"Relax," he said. "There's no hurry. When you're ready, all three of us will talk about how we're going to handle the situation."

"I'm sorry," she whispered. "I feel trapped. I

don't know what to do."

She dried her eyes and blew her nose. John moved her hair from her face with his hand, and then gave her a hug.

"Ready?" he asked.

"I guess so," she replied.

As he led her to the kitchen table, he glanced in the direction of Mark. Still standing near the door, the attorney had been watching his client with a mixture of horror and admiration.

"Come to the table, Mark," John spoke.

The attorney composed himself as he joined the two.

"John told me about your story involving time travel," Mark said to Rebecca. "I normally tell my clients to be completely honest, but in this case, we need to speak to the FBI along the lines of their questions. We don't need to take this in a new direction. Do you want their questions to end?"

"Yes," she answered.

"Then don't give them new threads to pull from the garment, so to speak," the attorney advised. "This could soon end, and it could end well for you. The DNA results support the documented statements made about you living with a cult in the mountains."

"But, I…"

Rebecca's objection was met with a sharp rebuke from Mark.

"Stop," he commanded. "Do you want all of this to end?"

"Most assuredly," she answered.

"Then we have to lay our bricks upon the foundation that we have already established. Your living with that cult is fixed in the minds of those agents. They want simple answers to questions, so we will answer those. The first question deals with who told you that your father was dead."

"No one told me," she said. "Realizing that I had passed one hundred years into the future, I understood that everyone I had known was now dead."

Mark helplessly looked in John's direction.

"That's not going to fly, and you know it," John told her.

"I promised you that I would be honest with you," she shot back.

"We are talking about what you're going to say to the FBI, not to me," John said. "You and I have a personal understanding. We are talking about the FBI."

"If I lie to them, I go to prison; if I tell them the truth, I go to the funny farm," she blurted.

"Mark has explained to you that we have to build on what they believe to be the truth," John said, attempting to calm her. "That's what we have to do. Do you understand?"

"Do you really think this will end with me living a life not locked up somewhere?" she asked.

"I do," Mark replied.

"Fine," she said. "What should I do?"

"I suggest that we establish the reason for you leaving the cult," said Mark. "I want you to pretend you are standing on the outside of this situation, looking in. What would you believe if someone was sharing this story with you? Put yourself in the position of the agents. Let me give you a possible scenario that would be acceptable to the FBI. It's widely known that many cults force members to relinquish rights of choice and are told what they must do. What if the cult was going to force you to marry a man who was not of your choice? So, you ran away. Even if you were to return to attend your father's death, you would have had to marry this man. You had been confiding with a female member of the cult about your plans of escape. It was she who found you and told you of your father's death. You refused to come back to the cult, and she promised to keep your secret."

"Do you think that the FBI would believe that?" asked Rebecca.

"It fits," explained Mark. "The FBI is looking for an explanation that makes sense."

"The FBI said that those people were murdered," added John.

"The FBI believes the dead man to be your father, but there is no evidence indicating that the woman is related to you," Mark stated to Rebecca. "It's apparent that your mother was no longer in the picture. It would seem that your father had taken up with a much younger woman. Why does something like that usually happen?"

"The first wife dies, and the man remarries," she answered.

"There, you have it," said the attorney. "I'm sure that's what the agents have already concluded. Now, why would both of them be brutally murdered?"

"How did they die?" she asked.

"I don't have the details, but I do know that there must be evidence of murder," he answered. "If they were stabbed, bones often show cut marks. You really don't have to know all the details. The person telling you of your father's death didn't have to give you that information. I'm asking you why a couple like that would be murdered together. I doubt they were killed while someone was robbing their home, because they were living in a teepee, within a communal cult. Think. What other explanation could there be?"

"Jealousy," she replied. "There have been crimes of passion, where jealousy was involved. Maybe a young man loved the woman, but she left him to marry the older man."

"Bingo!" exclaimed Mark. "The first recorded murder in the Bible was about jealousy. It wasn't about sex, but still it was a crime of passion."

"So, you read the Bible," observed Rebecca.

"I've read it enough to know that account," replied the attorney. "This is the kind of explanation the FBI is looking for. If you had told them this story, I believe they would have taken it. However, you refused to talk to them, so they now want to understand why. They now believe you are hiding something. If this was the true story, why would a person be reluctant to share it?"

"Fear," she replied. "Fear for oneself or for a loved one."

"Why would someone be afraid to provide this information?" Mark asked. "Remember to put yourself outside of the situation and think of the answer."

"It could be a case where that person was related to the murderer," said Rebecca. "A situation where the person was trying to protect someone. Like if my brother killed them because my father married the woman he loved. A person can kill, if felt betrayed."

"Exactly," said Mark. "I'm going to the office for a little while. In the meantime, consider what you should share with the FBI. I'll come back this afternoon to take your deposition. Together, we'll document a detailed account of what happened."

John escorted the attorney from the apartment. Once outside, he placed his hand on Mark's shoulder.

"Wow," John said. "Mark, I'm truly impressed. I'm amazed at how you were able to pull that from her."

"No, I'm the one who's impressed," he replied. "I completely froze when Rebecca held that knife. I can't believe how calmly you handled the situation. How did you do that?"

"My mother was suicidal," John answered. "I've done it a thousand times."

126

Chapter 19
FBI

"Thanks for coming in with your lawyer and Mr. Walker," FBI agent Wilson told Rebecca. "According to your deposition, you believe the cult disbanded after the murder of your father and his young wife. But you say that you left the group before they were killed. How is it that you were still in contact with members of the cult afterwards?"

"Sarah Moore and I had a special place that we enjoyed going to while growing up, especially after my mother passed away" explained Rebecca. "When I left, I stayed there for a while. She suspected that I would be there. Sarah brought me a change of clothes."

"What can you tell me about this special place?" the agent asked.

"It was a small cave," replied Rebecca. "I gathered broken branches and dead leaves to make a bed near the entrance. Sarah led her family there after the group fell apart."

"This is when your friend Sarah told you that your brother Jonah killed your father and his wife."

"Yes. The group had never suffered violence like this before."

"Did Sarah's family talk about a motive for the

killings," asked agent Wilson.

"At the time Jonah did this, there were only four families left. Some of the members had become disillusioned over the past year, and they abandoned the group. Mary Peterson was one of the few females near the age of my brother. Jonah was drawn to her and believed one day they would wed. My father, instead, took Mary to be his wife. Jonah was shocked. He told Sarah that Mary had led him to believe that he was special."

"Your brother didn't raise an objection to the wedding?" asked the agent.

"My father was considered to be an elder of the group," explained Rebecca. "If the other elders approved of something done by one elder, the action was not to be questioned. Sarah said that on the day of the murder Mary told Jonah that she preferred my father to him. He felt betrayed and became very angry."

"Why weren't the two buried?" asked Wilson. "Why did these people leave them to rot in a teepee?"

"I didn't know about that until recently. Sarah said that the members weren't sure what to do about murder. They were a group of pacifists and believed in love and trust. They had never considered murder to be possible among them. My father was one of the founding members. With his murder, it became apparent to most that the group could no longer function. Before leaving, they decided that Jonah's punishment was to stay behind and bury them, and then become an outcast. He is to be shunned. It seems that Jonah didn't take care of the burial."

"Has he been in contact with you since?" asked agent Jefferson.

"No, I haven't seen or heard from him," answered Rebecca. "I don't want to hear from him. This is not the brother I remember. I don't know him anymore."

"In your deposition, you state that you left the group because you felt you were bringing God's displeasure upon those people," stated Wilson. "What did you mean by that?"

"My daughter died. Then my husband died. I felt that I must have done something to anger God. When members of the group began leaving, I felt that I was like Jonah in the Bible. I believed that God's displeasure with me was affecting those around me. I believed my leaving would bring healing to the group. But that wasn't the only reason. Without Grady, nothing was the same. I felt alone, even in the company of my father and brother. I thought things would be better if I banished myself to the cave. Now, I wonder if my leaving contributed to my brother's actions. Maybe, I could have seen his anger and calmed him. I'll never know."

"What made you leave the cave?" asked the agent. "The group had collapsed. Why didn't you remain with your friend and her family?"

"After Sarah told me what Jonah did, I was even more convinced that my presence was a curse. I missed Grady, terribly. I decided to leave the cave and find the place where members of his family once lived. Not long after we were married, he wanted to show it to me. He was allowed by the group to take me there once. I was looking for stability, and that place was the only association with my late husband that was left. The place was in ruins, but I thought I might be able to build some kind of shelter there."

"Wouldn't you want to remain and look after Grady's grave?" asked Jefferson.

"The group believed in replenishing the earth with the dead," replied Rebecca. "Bodies are taken deep into the woods and placed unclothed in a very shallow grave with no coffin or marker. Often, they are dug up by animals. I didn't want to go near the place he was taken."

"Are there any members of your husband's family still in the area?" asked Wilson.

"Not to my knowledge. I had no relationship with anyone outside of that group. Everything was gone, and that house was the only place I could think of. It took me a few days to find it."

"You didn't want to locate your brother?" asked agent Wilson. "You grew up with him. It's hard to imagine why you would want to break the only family tie left."

"My brother has blood on his hands. I told you that he's not the same person. To be honest, I'm afraid of him. Jonah murdered our father, and the girl he had always loved. He's given his heart to the devil, and it's not like he's my brother anymore. He's dead to me, I have no one. I lost my daughter, my husband, and my father. Now, my brother is no longer my brother. What would you have done?"

"I would go to the police if someone in my family murdered my father," replied Wilson. "The group had its own laws. What was I supposed to know about the police?"

"If I may interrupt for a minute," suggested Mark Fairchild. "Until meeting Mr. Walker, Rebecca had never lived in our society. If you took a native from an uncontacted island and asked him what he would do in our culture, he wouldn't think about our laws and customs. He would behave according to his own. I don't think any of us could imagine the culture shock Rebecca has dealt with. She had no family to help with the transition. If it wasn't for Mr. Walker, there is no telling what would have happened to her."

"Ms. Johnson, I can appreciate your hardships," said Wilson. "That doesn't change the fact that we have two murders, and I am interested in finding the person who killed these people. I want to find your brother. Do you have a photo of him?"

"No," replied Rebecca. "Teepee living doesn't provide walls to hang pictures."

"I guess not," said Wilson. "How about a description?"

"We have roughly the same hair color, but he's taller – about five-ten."

"Age?"

"Twenty-four."

"Weight?"

"He's thin, but I don't know how much he weighs."

"Does he have any distinguishing features, any scars?"

"He has a small scar on his left forearm. When we were children, he slipped while we were playing on a large rock and was cut."

"What part of the forearm?" asked Wilson.

"On the inside. He tried to catch himself when he hit sharp rocks below."

"Anything else?"

"He has a beard," Rebecca answered. "All of the

men in the group have beards."

"I want you meet with a sketch artist," said the agent. "She's just down the hall."

Rebecca was led away, while John and his attorney waited.

"That's some story," said agent Wilson.

"Until Mr. Fairchild was able to get her to open up, she had shared none of this," replied John. "I tried several times, but she would always become upset and clam up."

"What made you decide to help her," asked the agent.

"I honestly can't put my finger on it," John answered. "It's not like me to take in a stranger. She just seemed lost, and I felt compelled."

Within thirty minutes, a digital rendition of the sketch was sent to agent Wilson's computer. He reviewed it for several minutes, until Rebecca was brought back to the room.

"That's not much, but we'll put out a bulletin on Jonah Anderson Smith with this description," agent Wilson told her. "Do you have any idea as to where he might have gone?"

"No. He knows how to live in the mountains. He could be anywhere up there."

"I have another question for you," stated agent Jefferson. "When you met Mr. Walker, he said that you were wearing a pair of black shoes. When asked, he said that they didn't appear to be hand-made. Where did you get those shoes?"

"When we needed particular items like cloth or shoes, my father would leave the group to trade hand-made items in exchange for them," answered Rebecca.

"Other times, he would take our dog to a man who had an interest in finding truffles. That dog had a remarkable talent for finding truffles. I never met the man, and I was never told his name. My father would be gone usually more than a week, sometimes two weeks. He was paid fairly well, and he would return with the needed things."

"Pecan truffles?" asked Jefferson.

"Yes."

"So, the man you're talking about must have had a pecan orchard," remarked agent Wilson. "That information may prove to be helpful. You'll be contacted if we locate your brother, or if we have additional questions."

As the three of them walked out of the building, Mark Fairchild turned to Rebecca.

"They'll contact me if they wish to press further."

"I'm just ready to have all of this behind me," she answered. "Do you think they'll call me back in?"

"Hopefully, not," answered the attorney.

While John and Mark shook hands and chatted for a couple of minutes, Rebecca retreated to the passenger seat of John's SUV.

"I'm sorry that you've endured so much," John told her, as he fastened his seatbelt. "I can't imagine."

"I've never felt so disgusted with myself," she said.

"Confessing to the FBI was the right thing to do," he replied. "What your brother did was terrible."

Rebecca sat in silence the entire way back to John's apartment. Once there, she went into her room. He didn't see her again until the following morning.

"Good morning," John said.

She returned the phrase without making eye contact with him. Wearing her uniform, she left the apartment without having breakfast.

Chapter 20
Found

John returned to an empty condo that evening. He found a handwritten note on the kitchen table.

> *John,*
> *You've been more than kind to me these many months, but I believe the time has come for me to strike out on my own. You'll remain in my personal prayers. Thank you.*
> *Rebecca*

"What the heck brought this on?" he mumbled to himself.

John immediately opened the door to her now empty bedroom. All was neat and in its place; all but Rebecca.

—•●•—

The following day, John found her working at the hotel.

"I promise that I won't keep you from your work," he began. "You left without talking to me face-to-face."

"If we had been face-to-face, I would probably still be living in your apartment," she replied.

"If I've done something to offend you, I'm truly sorry."

"No, I'll never forget what you've done for me. I no longer need to be a burden to you. I've found the courage to move on, and I have."

"Would you please, at least, give me a forwarding address?" he asked.

She glanced over at the maid working close by. The other woman nodded. Rebecca pulled a pen and pad from her apron.

"There," she said, handing him the address. "But I want you to understand that I am staying with a friend. Please honor her privacy."

"Of course. Thank you."

Rebecca turned away to continue her work. As John made his way back to his condo, his heart felt heavy with a sense of loss.

What happened? It's like a switch within her has been suddenly turned off. Something brought this on.

He called his attorney Mark Fairchild and told him of her departure.

"Honestly, her leaving is probably the best thing for the both of you," advised Mark.

"What do you think caused her to move?" asked John.

"My guess is that after telling everyone about her past, including a murderous brother, she feels uncomfortable," Mark replied. "She may even be embarrassed."

"Possibly, but I get the feeling that it's something

much deeper. On the way back home from the FBI building she completely shut down. She didn't say a word until she left this morning."

"Do you suspect that there's more to her story?" Mark asked. "Maybe she senses the FBI will find holes in her statements. It's possible that she doesn't want to take you down with her if she's found guilty of hiding evidence."

"I don't know," John replied. "I'm totally in the dark on this. I'm confused."

"You haven't been yourself since the day you met Rebecca Johnson. You've managed work, when needed. But other than that, you've been obsessed with her. It's none of my business, but I have to ask. Have you two been romantically involved?"

"You're right, it's none of your business!" barked John. "And no, we haven't been involved like that."

"When was the last time you went out on a date?" asked the attorney.

"So, have you now taken up the profession of being a therapist?"

"No way," answered Mark. "Over the years, I've begun to view you as a friend. I tried to steer you away from her from the beginning. I was afraid that she wasn't stable, and I was concerned that Ms. Johnson could negatively impact your business. I'm still very unsure about her stability, but you've proven that I was wrong about your mishandling your professional life. You're a much stronger man than I thought."

"Thanks, but I don't feel all that stable myself right now."

"If something happens with the FBI, I'll be sure to contact you. Just keep me in the loop, friend."

"Will do," replied John.

"I'm sure that you have a list of women in that cell phone of yours. Call one of them up and go have dinner. Relax a little."

"Maybe you're right," John said, ending the call.

---•●•---

Over the next three weekends, John went to dinner with five different women. He went to the apartment of one, but he brought none of them home. John couldn't shake Rebecca from his thoughts.

The following Saturday, he drove to the address she had given him. The apartment was in the south side of Atlanta, in West End. A house had been converted into a duplex, her apartment being on the left side. Nervously clutching the steering wheel, he sat in his car for several minutes.

I promised I would respect the other woman's privacy, but I can't stand this any longer. I have to talk with Rebecca.

He knocked on the front door, and after a few seconds it was opened by a woman in her early thirties. She was wearing a tank top, with no bra.

"We're not buying; you can peddle your goods somewhere else," she said, greeting him.

"Does Rebecca Johnson live here?" John inquired.

"I don't think she wants to be disturbed," the woman answered.

"I'll take that as a confirmation that she's here. Will you tell her that John Walker is paying a visit?"

"I know who you are," the woman said. "A rich man like you has probably been with half a dozen women since she moved in with me. To look at her, I wouldn't take her for a woman who knows how to make a man jump out of his pants. But it's clear that she knows what cranks your truck. I don't know what Rebecca done for you, but I'm betting that you still want some of that."

"It's not her fault that I'm here."

"What is it with you?"

"That's a really good question," he answered. "I'm not sure that I have the answer. Will you tell her that I'm here?"

"We've signed an official agreement," she said. "It's legal. She has to pay half my rent for six months, and there is no way that you're getting her out of it."

"I didn't come here to take your rent. Please ask her to speak with me."

"I told you, she's tryin' to sleep. Rebecca's been put on night shift, and she aint used to it. You wouldn't know. I doubt you've ever worked a job like hers in your life. The girl is worn out. Why don't you just leave her alone? Leave your number, and I'll make sure she gets it."

John heard a weary voice coming from behind the woman.

"Who is it?" Rebecca asked.

"It's that rich prick!" shouted the woman.

Turning back to John, the woman complained.

"See what you done? You woke her up!"

"It's all right," Rebecca said. "I'll handle it."

Rebecca stepped out onto the front porch, and the woman closed the door behind her. It was clear that he had awakened her from a deep slumber. She looked exhausted. Realizing her hair was a mess, she ran her fingers thought it.

"Has something happened?" she asked, her eyes squinting because of the bright sunshine.

"You left," answered John. "That's what happened."

"You didn't need to have me around. You needed to focus your own business."

"I'm capable of handling my business."

"What do you want?" Rebecca asked. "I have to go to work in a few hours, and I really need sleep. What is it?"

"Would you please move back into my condo? Just come back."

"Why are behaving like this?"

"You're driving me nuts," John said.

"Why? I'm out of your apartment. You know the saying. Out of sight, out of mind."

"If you were out of my mind, would I be standing on this porch? You're not out of my mind. Would you please tell me what I did to cause you to leave so abruptly? What have I done?"

"You've been exceptionally kind to me. But, I'm on my two feet, now. You should put your mind at rest."

"Why are you so displeased with me? At least, you can give me an explanation."

"This has nothing to do with being displeased with you," Rebecca replied. "Seriously, did you think a hotel maid was going to live in your exclusive apartment forever? That makes sense to no one. I bet it doesn't make any sense to that attorney of yours."

"This isn't about Mark Fairchild."

"I've certainly cost you a bundle with Mr.

Fairchild, haven't I? I'm sure word has gotten around to all your upper crust friends that you had a maid living with you for months. That didn't look good for either of us. It needed to stop."

"For some strange reason, I enjoy having you around."

"How can you say that? You really don't know me, and I've certainly been trouble for you. You've were even dragged before the FBI on account of me."

"That was due to your brother's actions, not you," replied John.

"My brother?"

"Your brother's actions have been his own, and I'm not associated with him."

"Neither am I. I don't have a brother."

"I can understand breaking ties with him."

"No," Rebecca whispered. "You don't understand. I don't have a brother, and I've never had a brother. I had a sister at one time, but never a brother."

"What? John asked.

"Your lawyer told me that I had to have a story the FBI would believe, so I made one up," Rebecca said. "You need to go."

Chapter 21
Acceptance

"You lied to the FBI?" John whispered. "Is this what you're saying?"

"I told you that I needed to be away from you, and it's the truth," Rebecca answered. "You shouldn't be involved with me."

"The truth?" stammered John. "First, you tell me about time travel, and then you tell a fabricated story to the FBI? Truth?"

"Since I took that oath on the Bible, I've told you the truth," she said.

"Lying about a nonexistent brother murdering your father and his wife, isn't the truth!"

"You're not listening. I said that I've told YOU the truth, not the FBI. I would have told them the truth, but your lawyer was insistent that I tell a story about my father being murdered by someone close to me."

"I don't understand."

"I know, and that's why you need to get as far away from me as you can," said Rebecca.

"What did you mean when you said that you've told me the truth since making an oath?"

"I told you the truth, but it's understandable that you can't accept it. I don't blame you."

"You're talking about jumping from 1922 to the present in the blink of an eye?"

"Yes. That was the truth, but it's all right. I really didn't expect you to believe me. You need to go back to your life. None of this happened to you. You're not cursed by God."

"Cursed by God?"

"I've accepted it. I don't understand why, but it seems that I've angered God in some way. You should know that I haven't lost my faith. I haven't turned my back on God. I figure that the only way that I'll ever understand why all of this has happened to me is for me to continue to pray to God. Maybe He will show me in His own time."

"Tell me again," requested John. "Just go through the account of time traveling again."

"John, you don't need this. I'm trouble for you. Like I said, you need to go back to your life, and I really need to get some sleep."

"I can't seem to go back to my previous life. Everything has changed since meeting you."

"I'm so sorry," Rebecca said, reaching for the door. "I didn't mean for you to get caught up in the storm."

John reached out and placed his right hand on hers. He pulled her close.

"If I was to say that I believe your account of time travel, would you come back?" he said. "I'm miserable. Please come back."

"I don't think you understand what you're asking."

"I do," he said. "I'm asking for the possibility of being pulled in for additional questions from the FBI.

I'm asking for my attorney, a friend, to believe that I've lost my mind. But I'm also asking to become part of the most remarkable event that I've ever heard. I'm asking you to convince me."

"You have lost your mind," she said.

"It's my mind to lose. Maybe it's the place. Do you like my condo?"

"Of course. It's the most extravagant place I've ever lived."

"OK, then it's me," said John. "You became tired of me."

"Now, you're being ridiculous. Outside of living with my husband, you're the most enjoyable man I've had in my life."

"You like the condo, and you enjoy being with me. So, are you saying that you would consider moving back?"

"I'll consider it," Rebecca replied. "I've warned you about the risk, but you stubbornly ignore it. You should stop thinking about me and begin looking out for your own welfare."

"Come back right now – today," said John, wearing a hopeful grin. "I don't want to leave here without you."

"Leaving right now would be a little complicated," replied Rebecca. "I've made a promise, and I don't want to break my word. I've told enough lies to last me for some time."

"Ask your friend to come out to the porch. I would like to speak with her."

"What are you up to, now?" she asked.

"Humor me; just do it," replied John.

Rebecca opened the door and stepped inside.

About a minute later, she brought the woman onto the porch. John brought out his personal checkbook and a pen.

"You never gave me your name," he said to the woman.

"Julie Strange," she said. "Are you planning on filing a complaint about me, or something?"

"Julie, I am making out a check to you for four thousand dollars," John said. "Are you willing to void that rent agreement with Rebecca, in exchange for this check?"

"Are you serious?" Julie asked.

"That's as high as I'll go. Your alternative is to hire a lawyer to come after the rent money Rebecca owes you."

"Show me that check!" Julie demanded.

John held it in front of her face with both hands.

"Hell, yeah!" she exclaimed. "I'll take your money."

She made an abrupt about face and scurried inside the duplex. She quickly came out with her copy of the agreement and handed it to John.

"Here you go, now hand me the check," said Julie.

"You need to write a statement across the agreement noting that it is now void, and I want you to sign and date it,' John stated.

"How do I know that you won't just put that check back in your pocket, right after I do that?" she said.

John took Rebecca by the hand and began to walk away.

"OK!" Julie called out. "I'll take my chances."

She quickly did as John had requested and held the agreement out to Rebecca. John presented the check to the woman.

"It's a done deal," Julie said. "But since Rebecca's my friend, I should be honest with both of you. This check is way more than the six months of rent that she owed."

"I understand," replied John. "It's worth it to me."

"Wow, little lady, you must be something else," Julie said, giving Rebecca a wink.

"I have another proposal," John said, pulling four crisp one-hundred-dollar bills from a money clip.

"You have my attention, sir" Julie said. "You're not trying to get your check back, are you?"

"I'll give you this, on top of that check, if you'll work Rebecca's shift tonight," John told her.

Julie pulled out her cell phone.

"I'll call the manager now, to let her know that Rebecca's not feeling well," Julie said, reaching for the money.

"This stays between just the three of us, understand?" John said, still holding the bill tightly between his fingers.

"Absolutely," Julie said, as John released the money. "Believe me, I know better than to cross people with your kind of money. My lips are sealed."

As John waited for Rebecca to gather her belongings, he stood next to his SUV. He experienced a short-lived conflict between his mind and his heart. Unsettling thoughts rose up, but were quickly overpowered by his unexplainable desire to have her near him.

I must be losing my mind! Rebecca has told

different accounts to different people – including agents of the FBI. Now, I find myself accepting the version involving time travel. I feel like I've lost control, like a moth heading for the flames. A moth does what a moth does, it can't help itself. It's like I can't help myself. Gone are the days when I was like the bird that fed on those flittering moths. How can I feel so at home with someone so volatile?

For the first time in his life he had become had become comfortable with instability.

Chapter 22
Deeper

"**Are you up** for going to the cabin this weekend?" John asked.

"I moved back to your apartment six months ago," replied Rebecca. "I was wondering when you would want to return there."

"Last week you told me that the cabin is your favorite place."

"It is," Rebecca said, turning back to the book she had been reading. "I love it there."

John had felt a connection to Rebecca from the first day they met, but he had come to a realization during the time she lived apart with Julie. Without her, nothing was right. It was far beyond the physical attraction he had sensed for other women. To him, there was something unexplainable about the feel of her touch. It wasn't like the thrill of a schoolboy first sensing the gentle sensation of a brush with the opposite gender. It was a sense of peace, an indescribable feeling of unique harmony. For months, the desire to take her in his arms had been building. John wanted her. He didn't want to talk about it, sensing that it would ruin the relationship. John stepped behind her chair and placed his right hand on her shoulder. She reached and took hold of it.

"I'm going to start packing," John said.

"All right," she replied. "I'll do the same, once I finish this chapter."

He lifted a travel bag from his bedroom closet and dropped it on his bed. John took a deep breath and closed his eyes. He envisioned the two of them sitting in front of the cabin fireplace, sipping cups of coffee. This imaginary scene was interrupted by a pair of gentle arms reaching around his waist from behind. With a soft nuzzle, Rebecca placed her head against his back. Without a second thought, he turned and kissed her. In a deep embrace, his hands slipped below her waist. He pulled her tightly against his body. He felt her chest press against his, as her breathing became deep and more rapid. John suddenly pulled away.

"I want you, but I don't want to take advantage of you during a volatile time in your life," he said. "You'd hate me later."

"I approached you," replied Rebecca. "Grady's dead. That life is gone. After you showed me that old article stating that Grady's wife abandoned him and never returned, I realized that there is no going back. History doesn't change. Over time, I've reconciled the fact that I have no choice but to focus on the present and future. There will always be a place in my heart for Grady, but I've moved on."

"Are you sure?" John asked.

"It's been a year since I met you. I've wanted you to kiss me for some time. It's one of the reasons that I left. I found it difficult to be around you."

"Since you've been back, it's been hard for me to keep my hands off of you."

She pulled close and gently kissed his neck.

"We'll take things as slow as you want," John assured.

———•●•———

"Are you sure that you have everything?" John asked, placing her bag in the back of the SUV.

"I have everything," she said, with a smile.

As they pulled out onto the busy Buckhead street, John felt her place her left hand on his right thigh.

"You're going to cause me to wreck this vehicle before we ever leave town," he warned, trying to muster a firm tone.

"You seemed to be in control, back at the apartment."

"I'm not sure, 'control' is the word I would use. I'm not really sure what came over me."

"If you'll remember, I started it. You were innocently packing your bags, and I instigated other things."

"From my perspective, it was certainly a welcome instigation. I'm not sure that you started it. You were separating yourself. You had moved out on your own, and I convinced you to come back to my condo. I put you in an awkward situation."

"Why do you think I moved out?" asked Rebecca.

"You said that you didn't want to complicate my life," replied John.

"You're a very intelligent and successful man, but you're a man. Men are so simple minded. I was telling you the truth. I didn't want to complicate your life, but do you honestly think that everything was about your welfare?"

"Now, that we're talking about honesty, what were your other reasons?"

"I would think it would be obvious. I had feelings for you, and I couldn't stand just living with you as buddies. I had to know if you felt something for me. You came after me."

"That's not fair. I wasn't thinking about sex when I came after you."

"Are you listening to yourself?"

"I missed you, that's all."

"I'm just an angel of purity and innocence," Rebecca said, mocking John. "Over the past two months, I've seen you looking at me. Do you think I'm that dumb? I was once a married woman."

"OK. Guilty, as charged. Was I really that obvious?"

"You were trying hard not to be. Women live most of their lives being groped by the eyes of men."

"I wasn't groping you with my eyes!"

"Now, who isn't being honest?"

"OK, I'll admit to enjoying the view. But groping?"

"Stop acting like a sap. You wanted me."

"I do want you. You were driving me wild back at the condo, but you stopped things."

"I wasn't ready to take it that far," said Rebecca.

"You once told me that your faith in God has never been shaken. Does it have to do with religion?"

"Partially. I'm not like a lot of women you know."

"I've never known a woman like you."

"I don't think sex should be tossed around like a baseball. I don't think it should be cheap."

"Nothing about you is cheap, and I never want to make you feel that way."

On arrival, he put the SUV in park and cut the engine.

"Let's get unloaded," John suggested.

He opened the back of the SUV and reached in for the luggage. Again, he felt her arms reach around his waist from behind. He turned, and their eyes met. John's right hand touched her cheek. She took it with both hands and kissed it. Tears began form in her eyes.

"What's the matter?" John asked.

"I should just say it," whispered Rebecca.

"Say what?"

"I love you," she said. "I've been stuck on you for some time."

"I've never been in love with someone. All I know, is that I've never felt this way about anyone. I mean, I want you – physically. But, I'm good with taking this slow, if that's what you want."

"What do you want?" Rebecca asked.

"I want you, all of you. It's hard keeping my hands off of you. But we can take this as slow as it needs to be."

"I'm afraid," she said.

"Afraid? I won't hurt you, if that's what you're afraid of."

"I lost my daughter, and then my husband. I don't want anything to happen to you."

"I don't believe we have guarantees in life. A lot of things we can control, but there is so much that's entirely out of our hands. Maybe it's fate, or maybe it's God – I'm not really sure. I can't live life being afraid of what might or might not happen."

"You're right," Rebecca said. "I have a tendency to allow things from the past control me. I should do the best that I know and try not to worry about what I can't change. Worrying doesn't stop anything."

"Whatever time we have on this earth, I want to enjoy with you," John said. "Whatever time we have together."

"I love you, John."

"I love you, too."

The two embraced. She pressed her body against his, as John leaned back against the SUV. She ran her small hands under his shirt, as his moved under hers. Suddenly, he scooped her up in his arms and carried her into the cabin.

Just as John laid her upon his bed, his cell rang.

"It's my attorney," he told her. "He can wait."

"What if it's important," she asked. "Take the call. We have the weekend."

"You're right. Don't move. Let me see what he wants."

"What's up, Mark?" John said, answering the call.

"Where are you right now?" asked Mark Fairchild.

"I'm at the cabin for the weekend."

"I'm guessing that Rebecca is there with you."

"She is. Does this call concern her?" "FBI agent Wilson went to your apartment looking for Rebecca. Not finding either of you, he questioned the concierge. When he was told that you were away for the weekend, the agent contacted me."

"What does he want with her?" asked John.

"He told me that he received new information, and wants to speak with Rebecca. I think it's best that we get together to discuss things before she meets with him."

"Is everything OK?"

"I'm not really sure, but he said that what was found has caused him to need clarifications regarding the account she gave."

"What does your gut say about this?"

"My gut is concerned. I think he's found something that conflicts with her deposition."

"Hold on just a minute," John instructed.

Holding the phone to his chest, he turned his attention back to the woman lying on his bed.

"It appears that agent Wilson has questions for you."

"The FBI again, so soon?" she asked.

"Mark says that the FBI has received new information that may be in conflict with your story. He thinks that we need to meet immediately to consider how to proceed."

"How immediately?" she asked.

"I think maybe he wants us to return to town and meet with him."

"I was really looking forward to this weekend."

"Me too," agreed John.

"Maybe he can come to the cabin," suggested Rebecca.

John returned the phone to his ear.

"How do you feel about doing a little fishing with me at the cabin this weekend?" John asked the attorney.

"That would probably be a good idea," said Mark. "If there is something that is to be caught, I believe it's best that I do it."

"Tomorrow?"

"I'll be there by lunch," answered the attorney.

John ended the call and turned to Rebecca.

"I wonder what the FBI has come up with."

"It's probably not good," replied Rebecca. "I made all of that up."

"I don't want to lose you," John said.

"I don't want to lose you, either. Like you said, there are no guarantees in life."

"I guess we'll just have to take it as it comes," John said, lying beside her on the bed.

Chapter 23
Concerns

"There's something different about you two," Mark Fairchild observed, speaking to John in private.

"What makes you say that?" asked John.

"I'm not just your attorney, I've known you personally for a number of years," replied Mark. "I see the glances. I'm picking up on the subtleties between lovers. I've just never seen this in you."

"We've become close," admitted John.

"I'm not surprised. After all, the woman has been living with you off and on for more than a year. You've ignored my warnings and persisted to cling to her. I sensed something a while back, and I asked if you two were involved."

"At that time, we weren't," replied John.

"Come on. What guy has a girl move in with him like this, without thoughts?"

"I don't know. Maybe subconsciously. It didn't really hit me until she moved out. I couldn't stand being away from her."

"Now, let's change the subject to the issue at hand," said Mark. "I don't want to hear anything more about made up stories from Rebecca. I can't hear that line of verbiage and continue to represent her. We're friends, but it's unethical."

"I understand," replied John.

"Does SHE understand this?" the attorney asked, in a firm tone.

"I think you made that clear to her when she began going down that route. I believe she understands that she can't completely deviate from her sworn testimony. Tell me, what are we dealing with? Do you have any clue about conflicts the FBI may have found?"

"They won't tip their hand on that," answered Mark. "The agents want her as little prepared as possible. I think it's time we discussed a few things with Rebecca."

The two men stepped back inside the cabin and found Rebecca slicing up vegetables. She waved a large kitchen knife when she made eye contact. John couldn't help thinking about the last time he saw her with a knife in her hand.

"I thought we might do shish-ka-bobs tonight," she announced. "I've cut up the peppers, onions, and potatoes. This will make two steaks in the fridge go farther."

"That sounds really good," replied Mark. "Listen, we need to talk about your testimony to the FBI."

"You've already told me not to deviate far from my original statements to them, and you said that you don't know what questions they will ask," she said. "I'm not sure what we can do to prepare."

"Let's talk about the known facts," stated Mark. "We can eliminate the most substantial evidence from our concerns and focus on areas that may be questioned."

"That sounds promising," agreed John.

"Let's begin with the fact that a dead woman and man were found in the mountains," Mark stated, pulling out a pad and pen. "DNA shows that you are related to the man, but not the woman. The FBI has determined that the man was older than the woman. These are their facts, and I don't see anything changes coming from this."

"So, what might the agents question me about?" asked Rebecca. "You said that they have new evidence."

"My largest fear is that there is evidence now pointing to you as the murderer, instead of your brother," answered Mark.

"I've never killed anyone!" shouted Rebecca.

"I didn't say that you have. But evidence has a way of sometimes pointing to people who are innocent. They may have located your brother, and he may have given them a different account."

"I'm not worried about that happening," Rebecca stated. "I think we should drop that concern."

"It would be helpful to find other members of that cult," said Mark.

"I wouldn't count on that ever happening," she said. "What else?"

"It's possible. They may have found a cult member who gave them conflicting information."

"I doubt that any member of the group will be found," Rebecca said.

"You're probably right. I'm sure those people will get as far away from those murders as possible, and there is slim chance that any of them can be identified."

"What else comes to mind?" she asked.

"You said that, from time to time, your father contacted people outside the group. It's possible they located the man with the pecan orchard, and he may have given them troubling information."

"A guy who digs truffles from his orchard could be talking about a man with a dog, but I doubt my father would have told him about the group," she suggested.

"True. That's a good point. Make sure that you don't go in a different direction from what has been stated."

"You really don't have a clue as to what they've found, do you?" asked Rebecca.

"It could be anything other than the concrete facts that I pointed out," Mark answered.

"I think it's time we started that grill," said Rebecca.

"I'll handle that, now," promised John.

"What can I do to help?" Mark asked.

"The meat has been marinating, but you could pull the skewers out of the far-right drawer," she told him.

As John stepped out the back door, Mark moved closer to Rebecca.

"I've known John for fifteen years, and I've never seen him smitten by a woman. You absolutely reeled him in. He completely swallowed the bait, and I'm afraid there is no going back for him. I don't want to see him hurt."

"I get the feeling that you don't care for me."

"I'm still not sure that I really know you, but I hope John does."

"About me reeling him in - I doubt you'll ever believe me, but I wasn't fishing. I tried to get away from him, but he came after me. Things just happened."

"Ok. But if you get the sense that you may be taking him down with you, I'm asking you to cut the line."

162

Chapter 24
Contradiction

"**Using dental records** from Georgia, we've discovered that the dead young woman in the mountains is really Amber Stevenson of Atlanta," stated FBI agent Wilson. "Ms. Johnson, this seems to contradict your earlier statement in which identified her as being Mary Peterson. Can you provide us an explanation?"

"Mary Peterson was the name she gave us when she joined," replied Rebecca. "I know nothing about her prior life. The group culture was based on trust and acceptance. She introduced herself as Mary Peterson, and I saw no reason to question it."

"She came to the group on her own?" asked agent Wilson.

"Not exactly," answered Rebecca. "Several members of the group were artists who carved wooden objects. My father would be gone for days, selling or trading them for things needed. He brought her back with him, when he returned from one of the trips. Being a single female, she was placed with the Moore family. Jonah was immediately drawn to her, and quickly believed they had formed a promising relationship. My brother was shocked when my father took her to be his wife the next year. I think you know what followed."

"Did your father bring newcomers often?" questioned agent Wilson.

"No. This was unusual. As a leader, my father's words and actions were generally accepted."

"Do you think his original intention was to make her his wife?" asked Wilson.

"I can't speak to his intentions. When she was introduced, my father said that he had discovered that she held the same mindset and values of the group. She explained that she had become disillusioned with the current state of the world and wanted to be a part of something she considered to be genuine and pure."

"No one questioned her after that point?" inquired the agent.

"No, there was a culture of trust and acceptance."

"Ms. Johnson, you may go," replied Wilson. "We'll contact you if we have further questions. Thank you for your time."

As Rebecca, John and Mark exited the building, the attorney turned to her.

"The FBI seems satisfied that Amber Stevenson gave the cult a false name."

"I hope that's the last I hear from them," replied John. "Do you think they'll run more test on the bodies?"

"It's hard to tell," Mark answered. "I believe this new evidence makes it apparent they're opening new areas of investigation."

"What do you mean?" asked Rebecca.

"I think the FBI is now looking for contacts outside the group," explained Mark. "If I were them, I would think the woman was purposely brought by your father to be his wife. In fact, I wouldn't be surprised if he had not already begun a relationship with her outside the group. I find it difficult to understand why he felt comfortable bringing in an outsider, if he hadn't already gotten to know her extremely well."

"That sounds logical," agreed Rebecca.

"I bet it was the conclusion your brother reached, as well," added Mark. "He may have felt that he had been played by both of them. I can see how he possibly viewed the actions of his father as destroying that culture of trust; not just of the group, but personally; and while doing so, robbed him of a woman he desired."

In the parking lot, Mark parted ways with John and Rebecca. As had become habit, John opened the passenger door of his SUV for Rebecca.

"What do you think really happened to those people?" he asked, as Rebecca fastened her seatbelt.

"I don't have a clue," she answered. "I told you that I made up that entire story. I know nothing about those people who were murdered."

"I'll have to hand it to you; you were exceptionally quick on your feet with your responses to the FBI. Did you consider a wide collection of scenarios in your mind before going inside?"

"I consider a good many things," she replied.

"All of this seems very easy for you. You're very bright. The longer that I'm with you, the more remarkable you appear."

"Just because someone is a woman, it doesn't mean that the person is a turnip."

John chuckled, as he closed her door and moved to the driver side of the vehicle.

A turnip, she's not. Maybe a peach - but a very intelligent one.

As he started the engine, he felt her hand on his thigh.

"Tell me more about how remarkable I seem," she whispered.

"I don't believe there is anything unremarkable about you," he replied.

"That's a good start," she said, giving his thigh a gentle squeeze.

His eyes were locked on hers. John had been with many women, all of them more visually stunning than Rebecca. With them, there was an understanding that games were being played. The depth of excitement was in the playing of them. There was something genuine he saw in the woman seated beside him. He desired to delve deeper. He was fascinated by her quick mind. Physically, he was especially captivated by her touch.

Physically, I want to take her. But not sitting in an FBI parking lot at mid-day. There are walls between opposite genders. Self-preservation mechanisms, automatically launched when first meeting a person, ensure that our most vulnerable aspects won't become injured. These are learned, and over time they become habitual responses. I've caught glimpses of the woman behind Rebecca's walls. I want to know everything about her.

"I think I'd better focus on my driving, for the time being."

"I agree," she said, moving her hand to her lap. "Where should we have lunch?"

"I know a little café, not far from here."

"I'm ready."

Thoughts of the woman sitting beside him raced through his mind, as John drove.

I'm also ready ... I'm ready to explore every part of her – body, mind, and soul. I don't really understand how she does it, but she absolutely takes hold of me. It's not what she says or what she does. Maybe it's how she does everything; I can't quite put my finger on it. Regardless of the inconsistences on the outside, I have a real connection with her; there is something much deeper than I've experienced with other women.

168

Chapter 25
Belonging

"**What are these** people yelling about?" Rebecca asked, while watching news coverage on the TV.

"There are two groups, Pro-Choice and Pro-Life," John began. "The Pro-Choice people want pregnant women to have the right to end a pregnancy. The Pro-Life people want pregnancy to run its natural course through the birth of a child."

"End a pregnancy?" she asked. "Do you mean that they wish to kill a baby in the womb?

"Yes," replied John.

"I've known women who dreaded a pregnancy because of poverty," said Rebecca. "However, I've known few who seriously wanted to kill an unborn child."

"I understand that the baby isn't aware of what is happening, and the procedure is handled in a humane manner."

"So, if I decided to gas you to death while you were sleeping, that would be humane and an acceptable thing to do?" asked Rebecca. "You wouldn't be aware of what was happening."

"I shouldn't have said anything," retreated John,

throwing his hands up in surrender. "I'm not a member of either group. I shouldn't have commented on the subject."

"Someone has to be a member of a group to comment on a particular subject? You can't believe that. You're an educated man. It's like you're afraid to have a position on the matter."

"What is going on with you?" pressed John.

"I found myself in this world eighteen months ago. Every time I turn around, I'm faced with a reminder that I don't belong here."

"If you wanted to go back to the city; you should have mentioned it. I thought you liked it here at the cabin."

"For such a smart man, you can be as dumb as a rock!" she shouted. "How can you be such a sap?"

"Calm down and talk to me," John said. "What did I do to set you off like this?"

He rose from his chair and reached for her. She pushed him away.

"It's not you," Rebecca said. "The entire world has become insane. I placed my hand on the arm of a woman while having conversation at a store, and she told me that I was violating her personal space. She told me that if I did it again, she would consider it harassment. I could tell that she was unhappy, and I touched her as a gesture to show her empathy. What is going on with people?"

"Today, you have to be careful not to offend anyone," answered John.

"I don't understand what has caused people to be so sensitive," said Rebecca.

"I understand what you're saying. There's just a

current focus on not offending people. I'm guessing that at some point people will tire of it and ease off."

"It's like people have become cold stones, lying separated on the ground. People don't even know their neighbors anymore. Walking on eggshells in public isn't enjoyable. I just don't feel like I belong here."

"You belong with me."

"I guess it doesn't bother you because you were born in this mess. Everything is nuts."

"Talk to me," John said, reaching for her again. This time she didn't move. He pulled her close.

"I know that much of the world is in a mess, but everything isn't bad," he assured. "Not everything is nuts."

"You told me about the Great Depression, which happened in the 1930s. I've learned that the world went to war again, and that it ended when the United States slaughtered over a hundred thousand Japanese people with a single monstrous bomb. Most of them were civilian men, women, and children – not military. Since then, there has been war after war. I remember what war did to Grady. Why don't people learn?"

"I hate to break to you, but I don't think humanity has changed all that much over the years," John answered. "As for the bomb that ended World War Two, I've read that using that weapon may have saved as many as a million lives of people on each side. The war needed to end."

"I know that there have always been wars, but I hoped that the Great War would make people think. I shouldn't have thought that it would matter. It's not just the wars – there are people using airplanes to crash into skyscrapers. It's the entire thing. People strapping bombs onto children and using them as weapons. This is entirely against human nature. Even animals don't sacrifice their children. The world has gone completely mad, and I don't belong in this bedlam."

"The people in the US don't do that," said John. "Americans would never condone that kind of barbarism."

"No, here we have women going to the streets to demand the right to kill their own unborn children."

"That's not the same thing."

"Isn't it?" Rebecca asked. "People here simply have different reasons. Maybe it isn't done very often. It's hard to believe that it's rare, because there were so many people carrying signs and shouting about it."

"Actually, I believe it's happening less than in the past," answered John.

"That's good. Maybe people are thinking."

"Maybe so," replied John.

"People seem to think about sex a lot – not just think about it, but flaunt it around. I can't believe what I saw on my laptop. That should be between a husband and wife."

"Maybe, but I would think that people have always thought about sex. It's probably true that people have sex outside of marriage a lot more today."

"Well, that probably explains why so many women want to get rid of their babies. If you're having sex, you're going to have babies. Unless a man is wearing something, a woman is going to get pregnant. Men have a tendency to not think, when it comes to sex. Maybe if science could come up with something a woman could do to stop from becoming pregnant. Women would be far more responsible about things than a man.”

“Actually, it has,” replied John. “Women take a pill, and they usually don’t become pregnant as long as they are taking it.”

“Why aren’t these women taking that pill, instead of yelling in the streets?” Rebecca asked. “Does the pill cost a lot of money?”

“No, the pills are fairly cheap. There are clinics that give them for free.”

“Then, why are they so upset? Why kill the unborn when the prevention of a pregnancy is so simple?”

“People have freedom of speech, and they believe in a cause. They see it as a matter of women having control of their own bodies.”

“Just take the stupid pill! I was brought up believing that people should take responsibility for their actions. Everything is just so odd.”

“There are certainly a lot of odd people, but there’s no law against being odd.”

“What is it with raising children, today? While in a store recently, there was a small child screaming to the top of his lungs about wanting candy. The mother threatened the child five times, but did nothing to back up her words. Finally, the mother gave the child the candy. That nonsense only teaches a child that a person is rewarded for throwing a fit in public. I asked the clerk why the mother didn’t take the child aside and handle him. When I said that the child may just need a spanking, I was told that the mother could be in trouble with some agency if she is seen spanking a child in public. The world isn’t the same. Children are out of control, people allow themselves to be filmed while having sex, movies are filled with profanity and gore, and there are incidents of men gunning down crowds of people they don't even know. This isn't normal. I'm reminded almost every day that I don't belong here."

"I agree that children shouldn't be rewarded for bad behavior, but I'm not a parent. Regarding the mass murders, things probably do seem to be crazy. I've heard the statement, "We live in a VUCA world.""

"Vuca?" Rebecca asked.

"It's an acronym that stands for volatility, uncertainly, complexity, and ambiguity," explained John.

"Acronym. Everything is an acronym, or some kind of silly picture that stands for a word. That laptop you gave me has little pictures all over the screen."

"They're called icons," said John.

"Why can't they just use words. I have no idea as to what all these pictures mean. People can't use words anymore. It's like we've returned to the days of cavemen. We draw pictures, instead of using words. It drives me batty. I think the acronym 'VUCA' pretty well sums it up. The world has become all of those things. You're comfortable living in this? You're good with this?"

"No, I'm not good with it."

"I didn't think that you were. The world is out of control. I sometimes feel that I'm living in an asylum. I'm telling you; I don't belong here."

"I think you're wrong about not belonging. I have to believe that each of us are here for some purpose."

"I don't see the purpose. It's difficult to be myself. I'm put in positions where I feel that I have to lie. I don't want to be that kind of person. I'm just here, and God only knows why."

"Maybe you're here for me," suggested John. "I want you here."

"I've done nothing but cause you trouble since we met."

"I can't imagine my life without you. I have never felt that any woman belonged with me more than you."

"I'll have to say that you're my refuge in all this craziness. I don't know what I would do without you."

"I don't want you to ever leave me," said John

"What are you saying?"

"I'm saying that I'm in love with you and having you here with me is the rightest thing I can think of. I believe we belong together."

"I love being with you," said Rebecca. "That part feels right."

"To me, it seems that we are two pieces of a puzzle that fit. Together, they make the picture of life clearer. I love you."

"I love you, too."

John took her in a long embrace. She held him tight.

"Would you marry me?" John asked.

"Are you serious?"

"I don't think I've ever been more serious."

"Yes, I'd love to marry you," she replied.

John kissed her, and his hands began to wander. Rebecca immediately stopped his progress.

"What?" John asked. "Have you changed your mind already?"

"A thought just occurred to me."

"What are you thinking?"

"I'm thinking that if the FBI doesn't leave this

cult thing alone, our honeymoon may be brief," replied Rebecca.

Chapter 26
Peace

As soon as Danny Moffato, head of the security firm hired by John, left the Atlanta condo, John turned to Rebecca.

"It was nice of Danny to drop by and introduce himself to you."

"I don't like that guy," she replied. "He looks like a rough character. I'm not sure that you should be associated with him."

"I understand that he was pretty tough when he was young, but my parents brought him on to head up security for the various properties a long time ago. I've been associated with him most of my life. When I was a kid, I called him Uncle Danny. I appreciate the fact that he cared enough to drop by the condo to congratulate us on our engagement. I'm not sure where he finds the guys working for him, and I don't ask. He's always done a great job."

"That's what I mean," Rebecca added. "There are things that you don't want to know about what he does. Doesn't that bother you?"

"Nope."

"He gives me the creeps. He reminds me of a gangster who would order his thugs to murder someone in an alley. He's been associated with your family for decades, and you've never mentioned him before the surprise visit. The relationship seems a little secretive."

"I don't think that I've had a reason to mention him. Listen, Danny Moffato is no gangster. His people are certainly effective, but I'm not ready to call his employees thugs. He attends a Catholic church."

"I need to find a church," Rebecca said, while diligently searching for one using her laptop.

"A church wedding is fine," replied John.

"Not just for the wedding. Would you be open to attending church on a regular basis with me?"

"I guess," answered John. "What brought this on?"

"I've been wanting to find a church for some time."

"Yeah, sure," answered John.

"You'll help me visit churches? I can't drive, so I can't visit them on my own."

"Sure, but at some point, you should learn to drive."

"I'm not driving a car in Atlanta!" shouted Rebecca. "I'm still nervous just riding in town with you."

"OK, we'll start out on the country roads near the cabin."

"Maybe," she answered. "I found five churches within twenty miles of the cabin that I would like to visit."

"Print out the locations, and we'll give them a try."

On the third Sunday of searching, Rebecca found one within twenty minutes of the cabin that John liked.

John agreed to visit it, so they made arrangements to spend a few weeks at the cabin. The congregation consisted of less than one hundred, and a few of them were wealthy retired Atlanta businessmen. John found them to be more interesting than members of the other churches they had visited. The pastor was an older man who had come out of retirement to serve this rural church. He had once pastored a large church in Atlanta, but moved to northeast Georgia for retirement.

"I liked the sermon," remarked John.

"I'm surprised that you listened," said Rebecca.

"I listened. The minister talked about investments. He said that each day we are given in life is an opportunity to invest in eternity. That there are eternal influences as we touch the lives of others, and each day gives us opportunities to show our gratitude for God's eternal grace."

"You did listen!"

"I think you liked the church at Blue Springs better," said John.

"That church was more like what I'm accustomed to, but I also like this one. Some of the people are rich, but they're not uppity."

"Does this one meet your criteria for the wedding?"

"It does," she answered.

"Are you ready to talk to the preacher about it?" John asked, while pointing to Reverend Bill Whitworth.

"I'm ready, if you are."

They caught the older man as he was locking up the church.

"What can I do for you two?" the minister asked.

"We plan to marry soon, and I wondered if you

would be interested in performing the ceremony," answered Rebecca.

"Would you have time to discuss it while having lunch?" asked Whitworth. "I can offer sandwiches, if that's OK with you."

"Sure," answered John.

After a short introduction, the couple followed the minister to his home. He invited them inside.

"You two aren't a couple of kids, so I'm not going to require pre-marital counseling," Whitworth began, as he brought a loaf of bread from the kitchen cabinet. "But I'm offering it, if you wish. How long have you been together?"

"We've grown close over the past eighteen months," volunteered Rebecca.

"I have turkey, ham, or peanut butter and jelly," said the minister. "I'll put it all on the counter, with the fixings, and you can pick whatever you want. How about sweet tea?"

"Sweet tea is fine, Doctor Whitworth," answered John.

"I have a doctorate in theology, but you can just call me Bill," stated the minister. "Have either of you been married before?"

"I have," answered Rebecca. "Not long after my daughter passed away, we parted." She carefully worded her statements, as to not lie.

"I'm very sorry to hear of your loss," replied Bill. "After my wife passed away, I found that this church was in need of an interim pastor. I needed something to occupy my time. The leadership of the church eventually asked that I take the job of Senior Pastor. I accepted, with conditions. Since I have retirement income, I demanded that my salary be reduced to one quarter of what was offered, and that they use the rest to hire a younger assistant pastor. I want no part of attending meetings, and don't feel up to making all the hospital visits. I leave those duties to the younger pastor. The assistant pastor accompanies me during counseling sessions, and he has the duty of preaching on Wednesday nights and on the third Sunday morning of each month. I want to use my experience to mentor a rising minister. That's my story. What is yours, young man?"

"I own several properties in Atlanta, but I'm able to spend a good deal of time at my cabin," answered John. "It's not far from here. At age thirty-nine, I'm a dozen years older than Rebecca. She's probably the wiser of the two of us."

"Do you consider yourself to be the wiser of the two of you?" the minister asked Rebecca.

"That's not how I see it," answered Rebecca, while giving John a wink. "John's wrong. I learn something from him each day. I don't know what I would do without him."

"Now, that's the kind of disagreement that I like to see in a marriage," said Bill. "Do you plan to invite many to the wedding?"

"Our parents have passed away, and there will be no family members present," answered Rebecca. "I expect the wedding to be quite small."

"That's unusual for you both to have lost your parents at such young ages," remarked Bill. "Rebecca, you've lost so much. Your parents and child are dead, and you and your former husband have parted. Do you hear from him?"

"He's since passed away, as well," replied Rebecca. "I know that it sounds like I'm cursed, but I've retained my faith."

"You're not cursed," stressed Bill. "You're experiencing what many others do, but in a much shorter time span. Hold on to your faith."

"I will, and I plan to hold on to this man," Rebecca said.

"You do that," the minister advised. "John, what are your plans?"

"My attorney, Mark Fairchild, is to be my best man," he answered. "I'm leaving the rest to you and Rebecca."

"I look forward to the ceremony, and I look forward to getting to know you both better," said Bill. "Rebecca, there's something special about you."

"What would that be?" she nervously asked.

"There is something about you that reminds me of someone who was very special in my life," began Bill. "You're a beautiful young woman, but your voice and manner remind me of my grandmother."

"Gee, thanks!" blurted Rebecca. "I'm Granny, now."

John laughed out loud, while Bill attempted to recover.

"I'm supposed to be the wise pastor. But I've wasted no time putting my foot in my mouth, it seems. John, help me here."

"I'm just glad that it's you, and not me," said John.

"Rebecca, my grandmother was probably the wisest person I've ever known," explained Bill. "Her influence on my life was profound."

"How so?" asked Rebecca.

"My mother committed suicide, and my grandmother was there for me," answered Bill.

"I'm sorry for making a joke," replied Rebecca. "You've suffered loneliness that no child should. I'm so sorry."

"You couldn't have known," stated Bill. "You and I both have suffered loss."

"Bill, we have that in common," added John. "My mother was finally successful in her last suicide attempt."

Within minutes, an unshakable bond was established between the three. As John dropped into the seat of his SUV, he turned to Rebecca.

"I feel like I just visited a dear old friend."

"I believe God brought us to him and that church," replied Rebecca. "That was absolutely remarkable. There was an embrace of kindred spirits."

Suddenly, Rebecca burst into tears.

"What's wrong?" asked John.

"It's like the curse I've felt for so long just lifted," she sobbed. "I really believe that God's hand is in this. I feel like a weight has been pushed off of my shoulders. To have your love, and now to meet this man…I'm truly blessed."

John leaned over and held her. Parked outside the pastor's house, they were bathed in an unexpected peace.

184

Chapter 27
Flight

"**I've never seen** anything like this place," said Rebecca, as she held on to John's arm with her left hand while pulling her carry-on bag with the other.

"Atlanta's Hartsfield-Jackson is one of the busiest airports in the world," he replied. "The gate's not far."

Rebecca asked that they sit near the window of the terminal so that she could see the planes. She turned her eyes from the masses of people flowing like a river in torrents through the concourse and peered out the glass.

"So many people; so many airplanes – and some of them are huge!" she said.

She watched in amazement, as large metal bodied jets lifted off the ground and pushed their way toward the clouds hanging over Atlanta. One after another, they followed the climb of the one before them. As soon as one disappeared into clouds, there was another ascending. Her eyes widened, as she understood that this pattern was occurring on multiple runways.

"My Lord!" she whispered. "How do they keep from running into each other?"

"There are air traffic controllers in the control tower," answered John. "They watch them visually and on radar, and they are able to talk to the pilots over by radio.”

“Grady and I hoped to one day own a radio,” she replied. “I could have never imagined it being used in flight.”

“Grady must have been a good man,” replied John. “I guess you still miss him.”

“That was a different marriage in a different time. We began to struggle financially in 1920. Cotton prices dropped, and they were worse in 1921. Things were sometimes tense.”

“I understood that the Great Depression began with the stock market crash of 1929,” said John.

“I can’t tell you about stocks, but Europe began growing their own crops again after the war. We didn’t realize it, so we planted far more than would sell. Everyone did. Prices dropped through the floor. Grady had taken loans for seed and fertilizer in 1920, and we still owed money.”

“Financially, I hope to provide you a less tense life,” said John. “But nothing can be guaranteed. I would think that most in the 20s never imagined the widespread financial difficulties of the 30s.”

“I plan to take life a day at a time, and I look forward to spending them with you.”

“I feel the same about my life with you. However, regarding financial matters, I have to plan. I have to anticipate business expenditures and where the market is going. But, I promise to put that planning on hold while we’re on the honeymoon.”

“The ceremony was perfect. I was really surprised when the women of that church gave me a wedding shower. I hardly knew most of them.”

The conversation was interrupted by a voice over the speakers of the gate announcing that it was time to board. They stood when the call for first class was made.

"As requested, your seat is by the window," John said, handing Rebecca her ticket.

Rebecca's eyes examined every aspect of the experience of boarding. Peering down the aisle of the plane, she was stunned.

"It's so large! I don't see how it gets off the ground."

She took hold of John's hand when the plane was pushed away from the terminal. Then, hearing the engines rev, she squeezed it tight. She peered intently out the window at other jets launching themselves down runways and up into the air.

"Well, it's obvious that they do get off the ground," Rebecca said, reaching for the safety pamphlet.

She listened closely to the instructions of the flight attendant, taking in every word. When air mask demonstration was performed, she turned to John.

"Why would I need an air mask?"

"The air is pretty thin at thirty-four thousand feet," he replied.

Her eyes widened, and she tightened her belt. Turning back to the window, she marveled at the line of planes awaiting their turn for takeoff.

"So many," she began. "How often do they crash?"

"It's actually safer to fly, than to take a trip by car," answered John. "More people die in car accidents."

"That makes sense. There are more things to hit on the ground."

At last, their plane was positioned at the runway. It was then that she noticed that the rain had stopped.

"That was a pricey breakfast we ate at the airport," Rebecca said. "I hope I don't lose it when we takeoff."

She heard a chuckle from the woman across the aisle. The engine suddenly came to life, and the plane accelerated. Her body tensed, and she gripped John's hand as if she was clinging for dear life. She felt the front of the craft lift up, and she peered out the window to watch the ground fall away. Soon, her eyes were fixed on the skyline of downtown Atlanta. Buildings of over seventy stories began to look small against the vast surroundings. The view was soon lost when they entered thick clouds.

"That was interesting," she said to John. "It happened so fast."

"Keep looking out the window," he replied.

"I can't see a thing for those…"

Suddenly, the plane burst from the clouds into brightness of a fully sunny day. Rebecca peered at a seemingly endless ocean of white fluff against the clear blue sky.

"It's how I've envisioned Heaven," she whispered. "I've never seen anything like this. The clouds remind me of cotton, but purer than any I've seen ginned."

Her hand left John's, and she fully embraced the sight of the graceful movement of white puffs within particular clouds which towered above the others."

"Those large ones are slowly taking new shapes,"

she remarked.

"Those are thunderheads," replied John. "The pilot will make sure we stay away from them. They're very turbulent inside."

"Some people are like that - beautiful on the outside, but turbulent on the inside."

"You were absolutely beautiful walking down the aisle of that church," said John. "Were you nervous on the inside during the wedding?"

"Not until the music started," Rebecca replied. "The man at the piano played really well."

"He should, for what he was paid."

"I suspected that he wasn't one of the locals."

"He owns a music store in one of my properties. When he was younger, he was a studio musician."

"Thank you. That was a really nice surprise."

"Since we didn't have a rehearsal, I was able to sneak him in," said John. "Mark was the only other person who wasn't a local."

"There have been several surprises, like the wedding shower."

It's a nice church, made up of good people. I have a lot of respect for Bill Whitworth."

The clouds beneath them became scattered. Eventually, they were gone – exposing the vast countryside stretching toward a hazy horizon. Rebecca peered down at the wide twisted river below.

"The Mississippi," informed John.

"Everything is so magnificent," she replied.

Her view was interrupted by the voice of a flight attendant.

"Hot towel?"

"Yes, please," replied John.

With a pair of tongs, John and Rebecca were handed hot moist towels. John showed Rebecca how to lower her tray.

"We're about to be given snacks," he told her. "It's too early for lunch."

Rebecca watched the land below change from rectangles of farmed fields to thick forest. Later the land became treeless tan expanses, with areas of lush green circles.

"Irrigation," explained John. "They pump water from underground to long irrigation pipes carried in a circle on wheels."

"That's amazing," she replied.

Eventually, she saw the land in the distance become rugged. She watched as snow-capped mountains came into view. Rebecca tugged at John sleeve and pointed.

"Those are the Rocky Mountains," he said. "I believe the flight will carry us over Denver. Soon, you may be able to make it out before we reach the mountains."

She squinted her eyes, searching for the city. Roads and buildings became more prevalent, and soon she could see the downtown area. She periodically glanced at elements of the city, but her main attention was drawn to the mountains just beyond.

"Seeing this from the air, I'm beginning to more fully realize the size and beauty of this country," said Rebecca.

"I've flown many times and to many places, but I'm still in awe when I see it," replied John.

"Thank you. Thank you, so much for letting me experience this."

"We have miles to go, and more to see," said John. "Next stop will be Salt Lake City, Utah. It will be our only change of planes on our way to Honolulu."

192

Chapter 28
A Scare

"Hawaii was amazing!" began Rebecca. "I was stunned by its beauty from the air when the pilot circled the island before we landed. The botanical gardens and Buddhist temple were really special, but I found the natural surroundings to be more interesting. To me, the waves crashing against the rocks on the windward side was more interesting than Waikiki Beach."

"The beach can become crowded," agreed John. "Honolulu is even more crowded than here in Buckhead."

"I enjoyed the view of that beach from our room on the thirty-fourth floor of the hotel better than being down on the sand," said Rebecca.

"I enjoyed the view of someone inside that room the best," said John.

"I'm surprised that you even noticed me, with all the mostly naked beautiful women lying out in the sun."

"Did I really seem not to notice you?" asked John, taking her in his arms. "As I remember it, I spent the first three days examining every part of you up in that room. You're the one who decided that we needed to get out more and see the sights."

"OK, you've made your point."

"I thought you liked swimming in the ocean."

"I did. I was just self-conscious when I came out of the water. I'm not used to walking around in public with so little clothing."

"I bought you a skirt, so you could cover-up after you dried yourself with a towel."

"You did. Thank you."

"I know you liked the side-walk entertainment at night. You told me that you did."

"I did, but the novelty wore off after the first few nights. The city is just so crowded. I liked listening to the waves when we dined at the restaurant on the beach. I'd never been to an ocean beach before. I can see the appeal; the sound is so relaxing."

"How about the food?" asked John.

"Great, but really expensive!" she answered. "I know that it cost a fortune. The entire experience was a chance of a lifetime."

"We're fine financially. We can return someday if you like. Or, we could see a different part of the world."

"As long as we're together," said Rebecca. "When can we go back to the cabin?"

"I have to spend a few days this week going over plans to remodel one of the properties. Once that's done, I can turn it over to crews to begin work. I'll need to return in a couple of weeks, to check on the progress."

"I thought you had several managers overseeing the properties."

"I do, for the day-to-day operations. This is different. I handle remodeling, selling, and buying new properties myself. Until the remodeling is complete, I'll need to check on things periodically. Over the next three months, I'll need to spend no more than a week at a time away at the cabin before returning to the job site. The schedule has to be kept in order to meet the re-opening date."

John's cell rang.

"Yes, she's here," he answered. "Hold on."

He placed the cell phone to his chest.

"It's the FBI," John said to Rebecca. "They want to speak with you. Do you want me to handle it?"

"They asked for me," she replied, taking the phone from his hand. John placed his ear near the phone, as she answered the call.

"This is Rebecca Walker."

"I asked to speak to Rebecca Johnson," stated agent Wilson.

"Same person," she explained. "John and I are now married."

"Congratulations," Wilson said. "We would like for you to come into the office and identify what we believe is possibly the murder weapon used on your father and Amber Stevenson."

"Why do you think I would be able to identify it?" she asked.

"It's possible that you saw it in your brother's possession," explained Wilson.

She placed the phone to her chest and whispered to John.

"It's the FBI, and they want me to come in and attempt to identify a weapon they believe was used to kill those two in the mountains."

"Tell him that we plan to have our attorney present during conversations with the FBI," John advised.

She relayed the message and handed the phone to John. He immediately called Mark Fairchild, and the attorney established the date for the visit.

———• ● •———

"I'm sorry, I've never seen that in my life," stated Rebecca, when agent Wilson showed her a rusty knife.

"Try imagine it without all the corrosion,' Wilson said.

"I've never seen it," she again stated.

"It was found in the woods, about fifteen yards from where the bodies were found," said the FBI agent. "It certainly could have been the weapon plunged into the heart of your father. The size and weight could have easily reached his heart."

"Ms. Walker has stated that she has never seen the object," interrupted Mark Fairchild. "You have your answer. There is certainly no reason to force her to relive the gruesome details of her father's murder. If you have no further questions, I believe we are done here."

"You are all free to leave," replied agent Wilson.

As the three stepped into the parking lot, John turned to his attorney.

"Thank you for coming, Mark."

"Why did he continue after I told him that I'd never seen it?" asked Rebecca.

"He's trying to pick the scab of a wound, hoping that new details will emerge," answered Mark. "It seems obvious to me that this case is eating at him. I'm sure he has more recent cases, but he can't seem to lay this one down."

"Well, if someone murdered my father, I would want a bulldog like him on it," said John.

"Since Rebecca is the only person he has in connection to the case, I wouldn't be surprised if we heard from him again," warned Mark.

"You don't think that he believes Rebecca had something to do with the killings, so you?" asked John.

"Like I said, she's his only connection at this point," answered Mark. "He just pulling threads, hoping a seam will open somewhere."

—————•●•—————

"Back at the cabin, at last!" remarked Rebecca, as she restocked food in the refrigerator and cabinets. "The apartment is nice, but this place feels like home."

"I've always liked it," replied John.

"There's a slight chill in the air," said Rebecca. "It's just enough to enjoy a fire. I'll go outside and bring in a few pieces of firewood."

She found no firewood on the back porch, so she made her way to long stack of wood covered by a tarp. Rebecca loosened the tie on the tarp and threw it back. She reached for the top log. Suddenly, she felt a sharp pain in her forearm. Pulling it away, she saw a snake move down the logs. She screamed loudly and headed toward the cabin. John opened the rear door and stepped out onto the porch.

"Are you OK?" he shouted.

"No, I was bitten by a canebrake! I need help!"

John raced from the porch.

"Let me see it," he said, trying to calm himself.

She pointed to the two small needle marks left by the venomous snake.

"A canebrake?" he asked.

"Some people call them timber rattlesnakes," she answered. "You need to cut me and suck the poison out."

He called 911 and was instructed were she should be taken.

"Cutting you is not advised anymore," John told her. "Tourniquets aren't used, either. Now, the procedure is to get medical help as soon as possible. I'll get you to the clinic in Clayton. Hang on."

He picked her up in his arms and carried her to the SUV. She protested as he placed her in the passenger seat.

"That clinic is a good thirty minutes away," explained John, as he sped down the road.

"I've been around snakes all my life. I can't believe I let one bite me. I didn't even see the snake until it hit me."

"I thought rattlesnakes rattled before striking."

"It didn't have time. I stupidly grabbed it while reaching for a log. It was right on top, but it blended in with the color of the bark."

"The emergency person told me that you should hold your arm low and try to keep it as still as possible," John said. "It's important for you to remain calm."

"You remain calm, and make sure we don't run off the road," Rebecca replied.

Within minutes the pain became severe, and her arm began to swell significantly.

"I have a funny taste in my mouth," said Rebecca.

"My lips tingle."

"We'll be there soon," replied John.

"I'm feeling a little lightheaded."

"Hang on."

By the time they arrived at the clinic, Rebecca was having trouble breathing and she was sweating. John opened her door, removed her seatbelt, and snatched her from the passenger seat. Rushing through the front door with her in his arms, he shouted.

"Snake bite! Timber rattlesnake!"

She was quickly placed on a bed, and a nurse ordered John to stand back. Anti-venom was quickly administered.

"My eyes - everything is blurry," he heard Rebecca say. "It's hard to breathe.'

"You should begin to feel better in a little while," a nurse told her.

"I haven't felt this bad since having the Spanish Flu," Rebecca mumbled.

The nurse turned to John, giving him a quick wink.

"I think that was probably a different flu," the nurse explained. "It's been a hundred years since anyone had the Spanish Flu. That snake did a number on her. It's somewhat rare that a patient's mental state is compromised by a snake bite, but it happens."

A doctor reviewed Rebecca's charts and listened to her heart with a stethoscope.

"Her heart rate is still a little high," the doctor stated.

"Is she going to be OK?" John asked the doctor.

"You got her here in time to prevent damage to organs, so I doubt there will be any long-term effects," the doctor answered. "Often the worse long-term effects include the medical bill. I hope you have good insurance. Anti-venom can be fairly expensive.

"I have the best," replied John.

"I'm prescribing pain medication, and she should be able to return home soon," informed the doctor. "Make sure that she takes it. She'll need follow-up. Does she have a family doctor?"

"Not yet, and that's something I plan to correct immediately," answered John. "I have a regular doctor, but she does not. We haven't been married long. She was added to my policy before we left for the honeymoon."

"Her chart indicates that she's twenty-seven years old. It's unusual that someone of her age and your means doesn't have a doctor."

"She's an unusual person," John replied.

John completed all the medial forms, and within a couple of hours Rebecca was permitted to leave. John helped her fasten the seat belt. As soon as the engine was started, he informed Rebecca of his plans.

"I called and set up a follow-up appointment for you with my doctor."

"There's no need to go to all that expense," she replied. "I've cost you enough already at that clinic."

"The doctor at the clinic ordered a follow-up," said John. "You'll rest a day at the cabin, and the appointment is for the following afternoon."

"You're getting a little bossy, don't you think?"

"I'm stupid for not already insisting that you have a regular doctor. I'm mad at myself. There's a pharmacy on the next block. We'll get the prescription filled, and you're going to get some rest today."

"Like I said – you're being bossy!"

"Doctors orders; you can take it up with him."

"I figured the other side of you might come out after we married," said Rebecca.

"There's no side of anything," John replied, placing his hand on hers. "What happened earlier just scared the crap out of me. Seeing you suffering made me angry. I can't imagine life without you."

"I can't imagine life without you, either," she said. "I think I'll take you up on the pain medicine. My arm still feels terrible."

"I'll be right out," John said, putting the SUV in park and cutting the engine. "It doesn't look like the pharmacy has many customers right now."

"I'm sorry for being so grumpy."

"I think that snake bite gives you a license for grumpy," he said, forcing a smile.

"I though agent Wilson at the FBI was bad, but I'll take him any day over that snake."

John's smile became genuine.

Chapter 29
Communication

"**What?**" **John exclaimed** into his cell phone. "What are you talking about?"

"Is there a problem?" Rebecca questioned, from her comfortable seat on a chair in the cabin.

John held up his hand to signal that the phone conversation was serious. He listened in silence before responding to the building contractor overseeing the remodeling of one his properties.

"I'll set out for Atlanta right away," John told him. "Please stay at the site."

Rebecca's eyes were fixed on her husband.

"What a mess," John began. "A body was found inside a wall of the building being remodeled. It was wrapped in plastic and duct tape. Construction was stopped because the police declared the building a crime scene. I'll be in Atlanta overnight. I'll have to meet with the police today and make a determination as to what I'll say to the contractors tomorrow. We need to leave for Atlanta immediately."

"How did a body end up in the wall of one of your properties?" she asked.

"Believe me, I'm asking myself the same question. Go ahead and pack for at least two days."

"I want to rest here. Maybe you should handle this without having to look after me."

"I'm not sure that I'm comfortable just leaving you here alone. I'd be taking the only vehicle. Even if we had another, you still don't have a driver's license. What if something happened? What if there was some kind of latent problem stemming from that snake bite?"

"I'll be fine. I think this is something that will require your full attention. I really don't want to go."

"Are you sure that you don't want to come with me?" asked John.

"Yes," answered Rebecca. "I'm still a little tired and relaxing at the cabin is what I want. I'll be fine. I have the land line here; in case you want to check on me."

"That settles it," said John. "I'm going to bring you a cell phone when I return."

"The reception is spotty here. The land line is better."

"I'm going to set you up with a phone anyway, and I'm also going to make sure that you're able to drive. I told you that we'd practice driving out here, instead of Atlanta. Instead, we went on the honeymoon."

"Are you saying that you'd rather teach me to drive than bed me in Hawaii?" Rebecca teased.

"You know the answer to that," John answered with a wink.

He pulled her close and held her tight in an embrace. His hands slid down her back and inside the rear of her jeans.

"I thought you were in a hurry to meet with the police," she said.

"I really don't want to leave you," he replied.

"I'll be fine. Do what you need to do there and hurry back."

John kissed her deeply, and then pulled away. Rebecca unbuttoned her shirt, revealing her breasts.

"Don't do that," he said. "If you don't stop, I may just begin pulling those clothes off you right here. I'll never get to Atlanta."

"I just wanted you to remember to come back," she teased, as she closed her shirt.

———•●•———

"What in the world?" Rebecca whispered.

It was almost dusk. Straining her ears, she distinctly heard a male voice outside the cabin. Taking a butcher knife, she quietly left the kitchen and made her way to the window near the front door. She peered out, but saw no one. She was startled by a loud banging on the front door, followed by a voice that she recognized.

"It's Bobby Thompson!" he yelled. "Tell this gorilla to let go of me."

Gripping the knife, she unlocked the door and opened it slightly. Standing on the front porch, was a huge man holding Bobby by the collar.

"What's going on?" she asked, the door still not fully open.

"Ms. Walker, I found this guy poking around your cabin," the large man announced in a deep throated voice.

"I know Bobby; who are you?" she asked.

"I work for Danny Moffato's security service," he

answered, pointing to a monogram on his shirt.

"What?" asked Rebecca.

"Your husband wanted someone to look after you while he was away," explained the huge man, releasing Bobby.

"Why are you here?" she asked Bobby, while fully opening the door.

"John wanted me to look over the stacked firewood, for snakes," he said. "He told me about the canebrake biting you. How are you doing?"

"I was doing just fine until you two scared the daylights out of me," she said, pointing the large knife in their direction.

"And Mister Security Man, what's your name?" she asked, pointing the knife at the large man.

"Larry," he answered, holding out a massive right hand. "I apologize for the fright."

She moved the knife to her left hand, and slowly took Larry's hand.

"Do you have a last name?" she asked him.

"Taylor," he answered.

"Is everything settled between the two of you?" she asked.

"Yes Ma'am," answered Larry, grinning.

Bobby nodded, while giving Larry a scowl. The two men parted ways. She went back inside and called John's cell phone.

"You need to communicate," she began, while watching Bobby from a window. He removed the tarp and carefully examined the stacked logs.

"Communicate?" John asked.

"We're married now!"

"I know that we're…"

"You aren't doing things only on your own now, John Walker. You have a wife, and you need to communicate."

"What is this about?" John questioned.

"I just broke up a confrontation between two men outside the cabin. I'm supposed to be resting and recuperating, but no – I have a giant beast holding Bobby Thompson by the collar and Bobby hollering like a little girl!"

"I'm sorry about that. Try to get some rest."

"There's no rest! Why didn't you tell me that Bobby was coming to check out the firewood for snakes, and there certainly wasn't any mention about sending a goon to look out for me."

"I guess I failed to let you know about both, and I'm sorry. I'm just trying to look out for you."

"I know, and I appreciate the care. But you've got to start letting me in on things that may concern me. We live in the woods, on a creek. I could have stepped out back without a top to get something, and there would be goggling Bobby standing there."

"You'd never do that," John replied. "I couldn't get you to wear a bikini in Hawaii. But come to think of it, I wouldn't mind seeing you naked outdoors. I kinda like that picture."

"Stop it! I'm serious."

"I am too. I'd really like to see that. Maybe I should put up a privacy fence, and you could relax nude outside."

"Just wait until you get home!"

"I can't wait to see that. I'm thinking now that I should skip tomorrow's meeting and come back to the cabin."

"Agggh!" she groaned.

"I got the point, and I apologize," said John. "I'm used to just handling things without consulting the woman I love. That has to change, and I promise that I'll do better."

"OK. Bobby's here checking out the logs," she said, peering out a rear window

"Good," said John. "Wait until he's gone and I'm back at the cabin before going topless outside."

"You're ridiculous," said Rebecca. "How long is that monster man going to be watching the cabin?"

"I'll give Danny a call before I leave Atlanta."

"That guy scares me."

"He's meant to scare anyone who intends to do you harm."

"He managed to scare the crap out of Bobby Thompson. Do you trust him?"

"I trust Danny, so I would have to say that I trust him also," answered John.

"I guess your mind's been occupied with that body found in that building. What did the police say?"

"They'll have to check dental records to identify the person. I was asked when the building was last remodeled. Records show that my parents did remodeling forty-two years ago."

"Do they suspect your parents?" Rebecca asked.

"They suspect everyone until they can piece together information."

"That body could have been there before you were born," observed Rebecca. "When did they begin using Danny Moffato's services?"

The call went silent for a moment.

"So, are you a cop now?" asked John.

"I was just thinking."

"Let's allow the police to do the thinking, OK?"

"All right. I guess you have your hands full."

"I'm fine, just busy. It's a real mess here, and I'll be glad to get back."

"I'll be glad for you to be back."

"I think I should begin teaching you how to drive."

"Thoughts of driving in Atlanta frighten me," Rebecca said.

"We'll begin on those country roads and take it slow."

"OK," agreed Rebecca.

"First, I'll need to put up that privacy fence."

"Good grief!" exclaimed Rebecca.

Chapter 30
News

"**Come look outside**," said John.

"What is it?" asked Rebecca, who was busy preparing lunch.

"Put that down, and come outside," he pressed.

She washed her hands and followed him to the front door. He opened the door to reveal a large truck in the driveway, carrying a white sedan on its bed.

"What did you do?" she asked.

"This is the one you picked out," he said, wearing a broad grin.

"You had this delivered?"

"Absolutely. Come watch as he lowers it."

She slipped her hand in his. The driver activated a lever on the side of the truck causing the bed of the truck to slide back and then lower in the rear. As the bed moved, John watched the anticipation in Rebecca's eyes. Once on the ground, the driver motioned that it was safe to approach the car. She moved toward it with John following close behind.

"It has the cream leather seats!" she said, clasping her hands together.

John had already paid for the service, but he handed the man a cash tip as the driver was setting the truck bed back in place.

"Are you ready to take it for a spin?" John asked her.

"Not yet," she replied. "It's beautiful; I don't want to wreck it. Take me to an empty parking lot so that I can practice with no other cars around."

"It's a deal," he replied.

As John opened the passenger door for Rebecca, the truck left the drive and onto the road. Before sitting, she slid her graceful hands over the leather seat.

"Oh, this is so nice," she whispered.

She dropped into the plush seat, and immediately buckled the belt. John closed the door and moved to the driver seat.

"It's so quiet," she said. "I can't hear the birds from inside."

John pushed a button on the dash of the CT5 Cadillac, and the purr of the engine could hardly be heard. He turned on the air and adjusted the mirrors.

"After giving the car a once-around on the outside to make sure there is nothing that can be hit, you should make the necessary adjustments inside before putting the car in gear," he told her. "After adjusting the seat for height, move it forward or backward so that your legs can comfortably reach the pedals."

"Don't you want to see how the car rides?" she impatiently asked.

"Not yet," he answered. "Before placing the car in gear, it's best to adjust the mirrors properly. As you drive, you should periodically check the mirrors about every fifteen seconds. Your hands should be at ten o'clock and two o'clock on the steering wheel while driving."

"You don't do that!" she exclaimed. "You drive with one hand, and half the time you're reaching for my leg with the other."

"I'm an experienced driver, and you're not," replied John.

"You're not a very good example."

"I know. That's why I'm making a point to show you how one should drive. The guy evaluating you for a driver's license will be watching to make sure you do all of this."

"All right. Are we ready now?"

"We're ready," John replied.

He dropped it in gear and moved from the drive onto the road. Within seconds the acceleration eased.

"Why are we driving so slow?" Rebecca asked.

"We're traveling at sixty miles per hour," John replied. "It just doesn't seem like it in this car."

"It's really smooth. Oh, I'm afraid I'll drive too fast without realizing it."

When they reached the empty parking lot of a church, he stopped the car and had her switch seats. Once she was buckled in the driver seat, he coached her again on the seat and mirror adjustments.

"You look good sitting there," said John. "I believe this is really your car."

"It feels really good," she replied.

"Now, put it in gear," John instructed.

She did, and immediately slammed the accelerator to the floor. The car sped across the parking lot.

"Whoa!" he shouted. "Let off the gas and apply the brakes."

The car screeched to a halt, John catching himself with both hands on the dash.

"Now, again – but gingerly," he said.

"I love this!" she exclaimed.

———•●•———

"We're heading to Atlanta to purchase your own cell phone," John announced. "I promised I would bring one back from the city, but every part of my brain was occupied with the issue of finding that body in the wall. Do you want to drive?"

"That city scares me," Rebecca replied. "People drive like maniacs."

"Over the past two months, I believe you've become a proficient driver. You have your license. In fact, I'd say that you've taken to it like duck in water."

"Well, I'm not quite ready to quack in Atlanta!"

"I'll drive your car, in case you decide to try out the side streets," replied John. "You may want to drive the neighborhood streets, as I inspect the remodeling of that building."

"You're talking about the dead body building," she said.

"Please don't call it that when we are around tenants."

"I understand that. I would be pretty creeped out if I was working late at night in a building that once had a dead body in a wall."

"I'm trying to move beyond that. Once I finish the review with the building inspector, we need to meet with Mark. I still need to produce more records to the police, and I want his advice before doing so."

"Did they identify the person?" asked Rebecca.

"Dental records match a cold case of a missing

real estate agent," answered John.

"So, they've solved the case. What else do they want?"

"They really want to know who planted the guy inside the wall and why he was killed."

"I'm thinking it had to be two people."

"What makes you come to that conclusion?" asked John.

"Somebody would have to keep the body in a standing position, while the other person walled him in."

"You've really given this some thought," said John. "Do you have plans on taking me out and hiding me inside a wall?"

"All I've got to say, is that you had just better watch yourself, buddy."

"Maybe I will. Speaking of watching someone, a crew is coming out to the cabin to put up that privacy fence. I can't wait to do a little body watching of my own."

"Is that all you think about?" teased Rebecca, raising her skirt.

"You're killing me!" exclaimed John. "Any higher and I wouldn't have to guess whether you were wearing panties."

She dropped the skirt and gave him a wink.

"You and your fence," she said.

Reaching the job site, John turned the Cadillac over to Rebecca.

"There's a cell phone store four blocks over," John instructed. "You know the carrier, and you have a credit card."

"A cell phone and your credit card. Now, I'm

really dangerous. What makes you think I'll be back?"

"The GPS has this location entered, so you should be able to easily make it back here," he told her. "If you have any trouble, call me on your cell. But make sure you're parked and not driving when you call. You wouldn't believe the people who are killed while distracted by a cell phone."

"Yes sir, boss man," she replied.

She wasted no time heading to a side street.

"Did you have any trouble getting back?" John asked Rebecca.

"No problem," she replied, holding up the purchased cell phone. "You were right about the map thing. However, I seemed to upset that woman."

"Woman?"

"Yes. Whenever I headed in the wrong direction, I heard the voice of a woman telling me to turn around. The map is fine, but I really got tired of her."

"You can turn that off," John said, with a chuckle.

"If we ever do this again, please turn her off."

"Mark wants to meet for lunch," said John.

"I think I'll let you take it from here," she replied. "I'm all OK as long as I can pick which streets to drive. I don't want to chance driving to a restaurant that I've never been to."

John took the wheel, and they met Mark at an Italian restaurant.

"How's the remodeling?" Marked asked.

"It's back on track after the delay," answered John.

"How can I help?" asked the attorney.

"It looks like the dead guy went missing just after my parents bought the property," explained John. "I've given them the open books, but I have private documents that they kept in a safe."

"What's private about them?" asked Mark.

"I'm really not sure, but I'm guessing they kept them there for a reason," replied John.

"I can look them over if you want," Mark offered.

"I'm reluctant to bring other people into the investigation," said John. "There are papers dealing with my parent's remodeling of that building. It lists the foreman and members of the crew doing the remodeling. There's information about other people, also. If I turn those papers over, I'm sure the police will hassle people who are now old and retired."

"Or dead," interrupted Rebecca. "People working a job forty-two years ago. Some of them are probably dead."

"Dead people have nothing to worry about," said John. "It's the living that I need to protect."

"Who in particular?" asked Mark.

John jotted down a name on a restaurant paper napkin. Rebecca glared at her husband.

———— • ● • ————

"I have news," Rebecca announced, stepping from a bathroom at the cabin.

John looked up from documents taken from the safe.

"What kind of news?" he asked, looking somewhat concerned by the details contained in those papers.

"You're going to be a father."

Chapter 31
Papers

"**Are you sure?**" John asked.

"It's the third positive test this month," she answered.

John dropped the papers and took her in his arms. Lifting her from the floor, he spun in two circles before putting her down.

"I need to be careful," he reminded himself.

"The pregnancy is not that far along," she replied.

John's cell rang.

"Hello Mark," he answered…."Yes, I've reviewed the documents thoroughly. His name is listed on the building permits…. I have no idea why my parents saved these documents in the safe… Do you really think so?"

John ended the call, and Rebecca placed her hand on his shoulder.

"What did Mark say?" she asked.

"I don't like it," replied John. "It's unsettling."

"Communication, remember? What did Mark think?"

"The only reason he can come up with for my parents holding these documents in the safe is to have leverage over Danny Moffato," answered John. "The building permits show Danny as heading the security service hired to make sure building supplies weren't stolen from the job site."

"The documents implicate Danny as the person who put that body in the wall!" accused Rebecca. "What other leverage could there be? Do you have a different explanation for your parents to hide those papers in that safe?"

"I don't know why they did it. I'm not sure that my parents would hold leverage over Danny. He's always been a friend of the family."

"You're the one who told me that he was a rough character when he was younger. It fits. Your parents bought loyalty from him with those documents, and the threat scared Danny Moffato straight. He became loyal to your folks, and they sealed his service to the properties."

"That notion is circumstantial, at best," said John.

"Why not burn those documents?" asked Rebecca. "If there is no reason to hold him hostage over something contained in them, why don't you just burn them?"

"I was thinking about doing just that before Mark called. Now, I'm torn. It's hard to image my parents knowing about a body being hidden in the wall and holding incriminating evidence on Danny in a safe all these years. This seem totally out of character."

"Deep inside, you know there's merit in Mark's idea," said Rebecca.

"That's not the only thing Mark found," stated John. "He said that the city doesn't have any records of building permits for the remodeling. Mark said that he is sure the police will look for those papers. These are the only copies. If they remain in the safe, there will be no reason for them to draw Danny into the situation."

"I don't know anything about building permits," said Rebecca.

"The Southern Building Code Congress International established building codes for Southern states in 1940," explained John. "Codes and permits have been around for some time. They were certainly in place during the time my parents remodeled the building. The permits kept in the safe have city approval seals, so the city should have those records. I can't explain why the city doesn't have copies."

"This whole thing sounds fishy," suggested Rebecca.

"For the time being, these papers are going back in that safe," replied John.

———•◆•———

"Why would someone stuff a dead real estate guy in a wall of a building owned by my parents," John asked Danny.

"How should I know?" the older man responded.

"The police say that the man went missing during the time when my folks were remodeling the place. That casts a terrible image on them."

"It doesn't mean that your parents had anything to do with that man's death," said Danny. "Anybody could have planted that guy in the wall during the remodeling."

"What do you remember about that remodeling? I'm sure that your relationship with my parents went that far back. I've seen photos taken before I was born of you and them together."

"Anybody could have put that body there, probably in the middle of the night. It doesn't mean that your family had anything to do with it. It most likely was the remodeling contractor. He would be the one in charge of replacing that wall. What makes you think that looks bad for your parents?"

"They owned the building, they were overseeing their building being remodeled," answered John. "The police believe the buck stopped with them. I've been questioned several times, and I don't see them looking at anyone else."

"That's what they want you to think. I'm sure they're questioning members of the deceased family member. For sure, they would be reviewing any of his contacts during that time. You have no knowledge about any of this."

"My guess is that they are particularly interested in people who were around at the time," John said.

"They've allowed your current remodeling efforts to resume, so they must have chalked it up as a cold case," said Danny.

"Construction has resumed, but this body turning up has caused them to reopen a cold case. They made us open up all the walls in that building, to ensure there were no other bodies."

"I'm sure they didn't find anything else that was out of the ordinary," said Danny. "I would think they would move on to something else. It's obvious that you didn't have anything to do with this murder. You don't have anything to worry about."

"What kind of position do you think this puts me in?" asked John. "Who is going to want to rent a building that for decades contained a dead body? I'm sinking a ton of money into that remodeling, and I doubt I'll ever get a return on it. Plus, it puts a stain on my entire business. I'll be known for this. A murder will be associated with all my other properties. This thing could snowball."

"In the long run, the visibility may turn out to be free advertising," suggested Danny. "You're right about it being all over the news."

"They've been questioning a number of people I know, and those associated with my family. If they poke around more, they may even question you."

"They did already, and I had nothing to say about it," said Danny.

"They even questioned my wife at my condo in Atlanta," said John.

"What about?"

"They asked if she had seen any documents in my possession which belonged to my parents."

"What did she tell them?"

"She called Mark, and he advised her to allow them to search the condo. She did. Afterwards they left her alone. She has enough to deal with. She's pregnant."

"Congratulations! That's great!"

"Thanks. Rebecca's wonderful."

"Those jerks shouldn't be pestering a pregnant young lady," said Danny. "That's just plain wrong. Do you need any help from me?"

"Did you witness anything odd going on during those days when my parents did the remodeling?"

"Relax. In this city, the police have plenty of current cases to pull them away from this. They will eventually let it die. You should leave it alone and focus your attention on the woman who carries your child."

"You didn't answer my question," continued John.

"You need to listen to people," stated Danny, his eyes narrowing. "Leave it be."

Chapter 32
Grady

Months later, Rebecca held her son in her arms for the first time. John made sure he was present for the event.

"He's beautiful," she said, glancing up at John.

"You're beautiful," he replied.

"I'm a mess. My hair is filled with sweat, and I'm exhausted."

"I see the two most beautiful people in the world," John said, touching the tiny hand of his son with his finger.

"I'll agree that this little boy is as handsome as his father. I love you."

"I love you too … both of you."

"I can see the two of you fishing at the cabin a few years from now," said Rebecca.

"I can see you rocking him to sleep at night."

"It's a deal," Rebecca replied. "I'll rock him to sleep right after you change his diaper."

"Not so fast. I believe we both will have turns doing both."

"Are you sure about the name?" she asked.

"Absolutely," John answered. "He's the man whose loss gave you to me. If things had been different, you might have given him a son. From everything you've told me about him, I have nothing but admiration for him."

"OK."

"It feels right."

"What do you think about the name, my little Grady?" she asked, giving the newborn a kiss.

She motioned for John to draw close with her free hand. She kissed her husband.

"I want him to have your middle name," she said.

"Tyree?" he asked. "Nobody has that name anymore. It was passed down from someone in my ancestry. I think it's Scottish, maybe."

"Grady Tyree Walker," she said. "Can we do that? Can we name him that?"

"Sure," John answered.

Four hours later, Dr. Parker Morgan stepped into the room.

"I'm glad I caught the three of you here together, I want to take a look at that baby," he said.

"He's busy at the moment," John said.

"He's already taken to the breast?" the doctor asked Rebecca.

"With a vengeance," she replied. "I don't know where he's putting it all. He's going to leave me flat and saggy by the time we leave the hospital."

"I doubt that, but it's really a good sign," replied Doctor Morgan. "Can you let him come up for air so that I can take a quick look?"

Rebecca loosened Grady's hold with a finger, covered up, and moved the baby within the doctor's view.

"We've named him Grady," she said.

"May I take him for a moment?" asked Morgan.

The doctor picked up the child and tested several reflexes.

"Everything looks good to me," the doctor said, returning him to his mother. "Excellent reflexes. Has a pediatrician dropped by?" he asked, picking up her charts.

"You just missed her," answered Rebecca.

"I see; Doctor Tate is a fine pediatrician, should you decide to stay with her," the doctor stated. "I'm your family doctor, but she would make a good one for Grady."

"I like her," she replied. "What do you think?" she asked John.

"I'm good with her," John answered.

"Well, that's all I have – unless you have questions," Doctor Morgan said. "I'll leave you to enjoy little Grady."

John accompanied the family doctor from the room. The two spoke quietly for a couple of minutes, before John returned to the room.

"What were you two talking about?" asked Rebecca.

"He's been my family doctor for some time," answered John. "I asked him if he was OK with not being Grady's primary physician."

"And."

"He's fine with it."

"What else were you talking about?"

"We belong to the same club, and we sometimes play golf together," answered John.

"Golf?"

"I told him that I didn't think I'd be able to play

eighteen holes, but I'd like to meet him for nine. Things are different now. I'm a father. I don't expect to have the free time I once had."

"I don't think you've gone to that club more than six times since we've been married," Rebecca said.

"You told me that you weren't interested, so I've become less active with it."

"You're a good man, John Walker," she told him. "I love you."

"I love you, too."

———•●•———

The following morning, there was a knock on the hospital door.

"Come in," Rebecca called out.

A vase of roses was followed by the face of Danny Moffato.

"How's the new mother?" he asked.

"You heard," Rebecca replied.

"John called me shortly after you gave birth. Congratulations! You're looking really good."

"Thank you," she replied. "I didn't know that he had contacted you."

"Of course. I've known him all his life. Heck! I even came to the hospital after he was born."

"Really?" asked Rebecca.

"Absolutely."

"I knew that you worked for his parents, but I didn't know that you were close to them," she said.

"I provided security for them, just like I do for John. But his parents and I were also close friends. I was over at the house a lot. You know, I'm John's godfather."

"I guess you were close to them," stammered Rebecca.

"You didn't know."

"We haven't talked about you that often."

"Really? Well, John talks about some things – others, maybe not so much. I care about John, and I look out for him. He loves you very much. So, that means that I care about you. You don't know me very well, but you don't have to in order for me to care."

"Thanks for caring," she nervously replied.

"Where's the baby" Danny asked, with a slight grin.

"The nurses bring him in and out. You just missed him."

"That's a shame. I was looking forward to seeing the little guy. Maybe next time."

"Maybe so," Rebecca said.

"John's lucky to have you. You make him happy. Good talking with you. I'll leave the roses right here. Tell him I dropped by."

"I will."

Danny placed the roses on a counter and put his finger to the side of his head as he walked out of the room. Rebecca waited a few minutes to gather her thoughts, then called John on her cell.

"We have to talk," she began.

"Sure, I'll be there within the hour," John replied.

"No! We need to talk now!"

"Are you OK? Is the baby all right?"

"Grady is fine."

"What's going on?" he asked.

"Danny is your GODFATHER?" she asked. "He

came to the hospital. He told me that he is your godfather."

"I told you that he's known me all my life."

"You get your butt to this hospital now! We need to talk."

"OK," John said. "I'm on my way."

Chapter 33
Larry

"**I guess I** failed to explain the close relationship between Danny Moffato and my family, and I apologize," John told Rebecca.

"I don't like the man; something really bothers me to the core about him," she said.

"Maybe that will change over time."

"Maybe."

"Listen, something has come up. I just found that I need to take a business trip to Europe to deal with an account there. I know that you recently gave birth to Grady, but it would be a great for you to see the sites. What do you say?"

"It's important for babies to have an established schedule, and Grady is finally on a solid sleeping schedule," she replied. "I don't want it interrupted, and neither do you. You remember what the first few weeks were like."

"I do, but can't he adapt to a new one?" asked John.

"He would be miserable, and so would we. Europe has completely different time than we do, so I think it's best that we wait until he is older."

"It's really an opportunity," John pressed. "Plus, I

would be worrying about you two the entire time I'm away. Are you sure you won't come?"

"I just think that he's too young."

"I'm going to really miss you," John said, as he rolled his travel bag to the front door of the cabin.

"I'll be fine," replied Rebecca.

"I know that you don't like Danny, so I've made arrangements for one of his guys to look out for you while I'm gone."

"Good grief! What makes you think that I would like one of his employees any better?"

"Humor me. Do it for me. If not, I'll be worried sick the entire time."

"All right, if I must," replied Rebecca. "Who is it, the huge thug that was sent the last time?"

"Larry Taylor's big, but he's not a thug," said John. "Give him a chance. I'll leave Danny's number on the kitchen counter. I seriously doubt that you'll have any trouble with Larry, but you'll have the number."

"I doubt I'll have any visits from Bobby Thompson while you're away. He hates that guy."

"He'll let you know that he will be around, and then you'll probably not hear from him. He'll scout the woods around the cabin during the day, and sleep in his vehicle at night."

"Sleep in his vehicle?"

"Sure, he's used to it."

"Come back to me," said Rebecca, stepping close to John.

"I'll make a point of it," he said, taking her in his arms. After a deep embrace, John left.

———•●•———

Two hours later, Rebecca heard a loud knock on the front door. She opened it and found the large man standing on the front porch.

"I'm here," Larry said. "I just wanted you to know."

"Do you plan to sleep in your vehicle at night?" she asked.

"That's no problem. I spent many a night sleeping in vehicles while I was in Afghanistan."

"You served over there?" she asked.

"Two tours, Ma'am," he answered.

"You can stop with the Ma'am stuff. My name is Rebecca. I'm sure you saw things over there that you'd never be able to explain to people here at home."

"Yes, Ma'am...."

"Stop that!" Rebecca cut him off.

"Sorry...Rebecca," he continued. "Special forces, I served as a Green Beret. I saw things, but I'd rather not talk about them."

Suddenly, Rebecca saw the human residing within that massive body. There was a profound sadness in his eyes. The same sadness she had seen in Grady after he returned from war.

"I was about to have lunch," Rebecca said. "Care to join me?"

"I have stuff in the SUV," he said.

"I have two steaks left over from John's grilling last night. I bet that beats what you have out there."

"Maybe, but you don't really know me. I appreciate the offer. I have what I need in the SUV."

"Come on in," she invited. "I can't promise a perfect setting. It's also time for the baby's lunch, and he sometimes pukes it up right away."

Larry chuckled at the unexpected statement. The top of his head barely cleared the doorframe, as he stepped inside the cabin. She could tell he was nervous.

Over lunch, Rebecca's opinion of Larry Taylor changed immensely. Within minutes, she came to understand that he was an unusually intelligent man and was self-taught regarding a variety of subjects. She liked his sense of humor. In turn, Larry was surprised that he found it easy to openly share previously hidden experiences with her.

"You're not what I expected," said Larry.

"How is that?" she asked.

"You're married to a very wealthy man. I expected you to be somewhat arrogant, but you're not like that at all. You've not once given me that impression."

"I have a sincere respect for those who have served in war," she said. "Thank you, for your service."

"I appreciate it. I sense that your respect for veterans is deeply personal."

"I'll just say that I was once very close to a man suffering from the effects of war," she said. "That relationship seems like a lifetime ago and talking with you made me feel as though I was talking with him."

"I need to be going about the business that Danny pays me to do," he said, lifting his huge frame from the kitchen table. "I'll have to say that your husband really knows how to grill a steak. Thanks so much for sharing."

"You looked like you needed a steak," she said. "You're a bit puny."

Larry chuckled.

"Your husband is a lucky man," Larry said, before stepping out the front door.

Over the next week, Rebecca and Larry developed a special trust and mutual respect. She felt secure.

OK, John. I'll have to admit that you knew what you were doing. Larry's not the man that I thought he was.

———•●•———

Danny spoke with Larry Taylor on his cell, as the large man sat in his SUV parked on the side of the road in front of the Walker property.

"You seem to get along with Rebecca Walker."

"She's OK," Larry replied.

"I believe that her husband, John, has documents in his possession that could cause problems for me," stated Danny. "I would like to see those papers. Drop hints about them when you're around the wife."

As dusk was settling, Larry was making his rounds. Rebecca saw him step from the trees near the woodpile.

"Do you need a blanket for the night?" she called out.

"No, I'm good," Larry answered, approaching her.

"How about a cup of coffee?"

"That's sounds good."

"Have a seat on one of the chairs on the back

porch, and I'll bring you out a cup," Rebecca said.

The big man took a seat as she stepped inside. Moments later, she returned carrying two cups of coffee. She gave him one and took the chair across from Larry.

"It feels good with the sun going down," she said.

"This is a really nice place," said Larry. "I bet there's fish in that creek."

"There are. John fishes there from time to time. If his business didn't take him places, I think that he wouldn't mind moving here on a permanent basis."

"How has your day been? Some new mothers are exhausted from little sleep. I hear newborns want to be fed every couple of hours."

"It was better today. Thanks."

"Listen, it's none of my business – but Danny said that he was somewhat troubled about some papers that your husband may have. What's that about?"

Rebecca flashed a glare in the direction of the broad-shouldered man. She scanned his countenance, in an attempt to ascertain whether he had knowledge about the subject. She quickly determined that he was simply a messenger.

"John has all kinds of papers in his business," Rebecca answered. "And you are right, John's papers are none of your business."

"I'm sorry," he said, rising from his seat. "I've overstepped."

"Sit down and enjoy the cup of coffee," replied Rebecca. "Do you fish much?"

"Not as much as I'd like to," he answered. "This coffee is really smooth."

"John has expensive tastes."

"I believe he does."

Rebecca could easily read the nervous tension residing in Larry.

"Relax, Larry," she said. "I have nothing against you. Danny placed you in an awkward position by prodding you about documents"

"I won't ask again," he said, sitting back down. "Thanks for the coffee."

Larry rose from the chair and handed her the empty cup.

"Have a good evening, Larry,' Rebecca said.

She watched him walk into the woods surrounding the cabin. She finished her cup in silence, listening to crickets sing a welcoming song to the approaching darkness. Rebecca entered the cabin and found Danny's number on the counter.

"Danny?" she asked, when he answered.

"Yes, this is Danny."

"This is Rebecca Walker. If you want to know something about any of John's documents, I suggest that you ask him face-to-face."

"What documents are ...."

"Cut it out!" she barked at Danny. "Don't sit there like a coward and send in an American hero to do your sneaky bidding."

"You must be taking about Larry Taylor. He served his country well. What did Larry say to you?"

"If you want information from John, be up front and talk to him about it."

"Sure, I'll make sure no one bothers you about papers," Danny answered.

"Good," replied Rebecca, her anger still boiling. "Don't bother me with this again. John may not see you for who you are, because of his lifelong relationship with you. But you don't fool me."

"I've known John his entire life, and I hoped that you and I would have a good relationship. Why are you so angry?"

"I hate sneaks! Don't pull your sneaky garbage with me. I don't like it one bit, and I don't trust people who behave like that. It's disrespectful and dishonest. I'm not your old family friend. I see you."

"Whoa! I've been kind to you."

"If you approach me through anyone again about papers, I may suggest that John and I have a thorough examination of all documentation concerning you. If we see something dirty about you, maybe it would open his eyes. I won't hesitate suggesting that he expose you for who you are."

"Are you trying to threaten me?" asked Danny.

"I'm just telling you that I don't intend to take any crap from you. Do you understand?"

"You shouldn't view me as an enemy," said Danny.

Rebecca heard something deeply unsettling in the older man's tone. She lay awake for hours that evening before falling into a troubled sleep.

I can't stand that guy, but it's possible that I should have just told John about this. The call to Danny Moffato may have been a mistake.

Chapter 34
Tension

"Larry, I asked you to do one simple task, and you blew it!" exploded Danny. "What exactly did you say to that woman?"

"I asked Rebecca if John was keeping papers relating to you," answered Larry.

"You're a moron. I wanted you to be somewhat subtle, not blurt that out! Now, that bitch thinks I'm up to no good and hates my guts."

"Bitch? Wait a minute."

"John married her, not me. She's bad for him."

"Bad for him, or bad for you?"

"You don't know crap! You've been working for me for two years, and if you cop an attitude with me – I'll send you packing in a second."

"That wouldn't be suspicious, would it?"

"You stirred up a hornet's nest with that woman. This wasn't supposed to be a big deal. I just wanted you to drop a few hints about paperwork concerning me – that's all.

"What are you up to?" asked Larry. "If you have a beef with John Walker, talk to him about it. You've known the guy his entire life."

"You sound like her! For such a tough guy, you

can be a real wuss. Maybe you two should start a knitting club, or something."

"I like her."

"You would. You probably would like to get in her pants."

"That's enough!" Larry warned.

"Or what? What are you going to do? Go crying to Rebecca? What's wrong with you?"

"Cool it."

"Don't forget that I have stuff on you," reminded Danny. "You're no choirboy. You may have fooled that stupid woman of John's, but I know the truth about you. I know what you did in Afghanistan."

"I was cleared," said Larry. "Mistakes were made. Stuff like that happens in war. I'm the one who has to live with it."

"Well, Miss Rebecca would have a different view of you entirely if she knew."

"I think you underestimate her. She's anything but naïve."

"She's a pain in my butt, and so are you," said Danny. "I've got to figure out a different angle, now that you've screwed everything up."

"I don't get this. You're the guy's godfather, he loves you like an uncle. Just talk to him."

"I can't now. I'm sure that woman has given John an earful about me. She's put me in a bad place with him. He and I have always been close, but she's poison."

"You're all about having stuff on people. It sounds to me that John may have something on you. Is that it? Is that why you're so interested in his papers?"

"It's none of your business. You're an outsider,

and so is the wifey. Neither of you should poke your noses where they don't belong."

"If you'll remember, you're the one who set me up to poke around. You did this, not me."

"Getting a little ballsy, are we? Who do you think you are? I have a lot of people working for me. I could disappear you in a heartbeat. Do you doubt me?"

"I'm not sure that I would put anything past you," answered Larry.

"You should never forget that. I have plans. You could be a big part of them, but you can't be stupid. You have to handle things subtly. You can't be noticed, because it causes me to be noticed. Do you understand?"

"I've got it."

"Good. Now, follow through the next time I give you something to do."

"Ok," said Larry.

"You seem to be on the inside with John's woman. I may be able to use that. But you have to work it."

"What are you up to?" asked Larry.

"That's not for you to know. Just do as you're told, and you could have a future."

"Rebecca Walker's not stupid. If I start playing games with her, she'll smell it out quick."

"If that's the case, she may be too smart for her own good. That woman is not going to get in my way."

"She and John are tight. I'm telling you. If you mess with her, you would be messing with him."

"I'm not sure what got into his head with her. She's a nobody, from nowhere. I'm not sure how she got her claws in him. I don't understand why he let his guard down with her. She's not good for him, and she certainly isn't good for me."

"I doubt Walker was thinking about you, when he married her," said Larry.

"It doesn't appear that he was thinking, at all," replied Danny. "See if you can finesse a little with her. She likes you. She called you the big war hero. She doesn't have a clue."

"I don't think I would be able to go there again with her. That bridge is burned. She'll be looking for me to poke around about those papers. You should probably leave her out of whatever you want to do."

"Maybe so, but it complicates things."

"Maybe you should deal with John directly."

"You really don't know what you're talking about. I have to be very careful not to rock the boat with John. I don't expect you to understand. I have to work around him."

"Well, Rebecca's not your avenue. That door has shut. She and John are tight, really tight."

"She's not good for him, and she's a pain in my butt," said Danny. "John could do better. Maybe he should do better."

Chapter 35
Silence

"The color of the main bathroom is strictly masculine," Rebecca complained. "Grady is three-years-old, and I've hated that color since the time of my morning sickness."

"You're certainly welcome to have it repainted," replied John. "For most of the life of this cabin, its inhabitants consisted of mainly me. I guess I've never thought about it."

"Of course not, you're a man. I don't need to hire a painter. I'm perfectly capable of painting it, myself."

"Go for it," John said. "Are there other masculine aspects of this cabin that need to be addressed?"

"I'd like to brighten up our bedroom at some point, but that can wait," answered Rebecca. "Female visitors see the main bathroom, and I'd like to give it a different feel. Sally and I talked about it the other day."

"Sally, from the café, is now an interior decorator?" teased John.

"Don't be ridiculous. A couple of the women from the church visit periodically at the cabin, but she's the only woman who comes to see me on a regular basis. She loves that cabin, but we both agreed that it lacked a feminine touch."

John laid the book he was reading on an end table and rose from the chair. He took Rebecca in his arms.

"I love it when you give me your feminine touch," he said.

"Is that all you think about?" she asked. "I'm serious."

John lowered his hands and gave her backside a squeeze.

"Grady could come in here any minute," she protested.

"He's three years old," John replied. "What harm is there in him understanding that his father loves Mommy."

"I just don't want to hear about him grabbing a little girl's butt while in the church nursery," she explained. "We have to consider things like that. You two are inseparable, and he mimics everything you do."

"We're in Atlanta. He'll forget all about me giving you a squeeze by the time we go back to the country."

"No, he won't. He's at an age where he thinks butts are funny. Believe me, it would be locked into his memory. He doesn't forget anything."

"I'll have to say that he's really smart for his age."

"Doctor Tate said that we should consider having him tested. She believes he could be a gifted child."

"Maybe we should put him down for a nap," suggested John, giving Rebecca another squeeze.

She removed his hands just as little Grady sped into the main room of the condo. He carried a toy airplane.

"The elevators on this plane don't work," he complained. "The pilot would never be able to control it."

"Let me see," said John, releasing his wife.

John dropped to one knee, so that he was eye-level with his young son. Taking the toy, he examined it.

"I see, Grady. You're right, but this is just a toy. No pilot would fly a plane this small."

"Of course not!" Grady blurted. "But toys should help kids learn, and this one is teaching wrong things. It leads people to think that moving elevators aren't necessary, when they are."

"Maybe I can find a remote-control plane that would have more of the functioning parts," suggested John. "We probably wouldn't be able to fly it in the city, but maybe Bobby Thompson would let us use one of his fields. Would you like that?"

Grady threw his arms around his father's neck. John stood, lifting his son.

"We could place this toy plane on a shelf," suggested John. "It shows most of the parts, they just don't all work."

"OK," said Grady.

John lowered him back to the floor, and Grady raced off to his bedroom.

"He's fascinated by airplanes," said Rebecca. "You taught him how several of their parts work, and lately that's all he can think about."

"He has the entire children's book on the subject memorized," replied John. "It's not just his capacity for memory, I believe he is beginning to read on his own."

"He's only three. I don't know of other three-year-old kids who read. I think you may be stretching it a little."

"I'm not kidding. I began to read the new book about cars to him, and he called out some of the words before I read them to him. He may not understand phonics, but I think he's memorized several words. Maybe you should take Doctor Tate's advice, and have Grady tested."

"Ok, I may bring it up at his next checkup," replied Rebecca. "Back to the subject of the cabin bathroom: I'll go to the paint store and bring home a few samples for you to look over."

"I trust your judgement about the paint. You don't need my approval of paint color."

"I want to share this with you. I want you to see what I have in mind."

"All right," John said. "Just a couple of years ago you would have never driven through Atlanta to a paint store. Today, you're a better driver than me. You certainly aren't dependent on me anymore."

"You're wrong. I am just as dependent on your love as when we first married. I don't know what I would do without you."

She embraced her husband, and immediately his hands again wandered.

"So, is it time for Grady's nap?" John asked.

"Another hour," she replied. She nuzzled and kissed his neck.

"If you start this engine, it's not going to idle for another hour," he warned.

"Are you sure that you don't want to take Grady to the cabin with you?" John asked, placing his cell phone in his pocket.

"Not while I'm painting!" she said. "He's so curious about everything, he'll get into the paint and have it all over himself and everything else. What was that call about?"

"It seems that one of my properties has been grossly mismanaged. I'll need to go into the office for a little while today. The meeting shouldn't take more than an hour, and my admin loves having Grady visit with her. He'll be fine hanging out with my administrative assistant, Jody, during the meeting."

"I like Jody. It's so sad that she can't have kids. She would be a wonderful mother."

"Call me when you get to the cabin."

"You worry too much, but I'll call."

A half hour after Rebecca left for the cabin, John and Grady headed for the office. As the two approached Jody, she held out her arms for Grady. He ran to her.

"Grady!" she said, giving him a hug. "I see that you have a book. Are you going to share it with me?"

"Sure, it's about volcanoes," he replied.

John's cell phone rang. He motioned to Jody that he needed to take the call.

"Agent Wilson," John answered.

"I would like to speak to your wife, Rebecca," the FBI agent began. "Is she around?"

"No, she is in route to the cabin to do a little painting. What's this about?"

"We have additional information about the man we found dead in the mountains a few years ago – you know, her father," explained Wilson. "We need to speak with Rebecca. Will she be back soon, or should I go out to your cabin to see her?"

"It sounds like this information is important," replied John. "Can you tell me what it's about?"

"We would rather talk to her in person."

"She doesn't plan to be back for several days. She's painting a bathroom, and my son and I plan to join her tomorrow. Our plan was to spend a week at the cabin."

"This should not wait a week," Wilson stated. "If you'll give me the address of the cabin, I'll go there today."

"I want our attorney to be present during your visit. I'd like for you to hold off until I can reach him. Afterwards, I'll call you back and give you the address."

"I'll expect your call within a couple of hours," Wilson said. "I won't wait any longer."

"Thank you," replied John.

As soon as the call ended, Jody spoke.

"Is something wrong?"

"I need to handle something before attending the meeting," John answered. "I'm going to my office for a few minutes. Please tell the others that I'll be a little late."

"Of course," she said.

She took Grady's hand and headed for the conference room. John bolted for his office. Once there, he called Mark Fairchild.

"Mark, I need for you to head immediately to my cabin."

"Hold on, what's going on?" Mark questioned.

"Rebecca is on her way to the cabin, and the FBI want to go there to question her. Agent Wilson told me that they have new information about the murder of her father, and they won't wait for her to return next week."

"I have an appointment in two hours," replied Mark. "Did the FBI say why this can't wait?"

"No. Wilson wouldn't tell me anything. I have a feeling that they've found something that might cause her story to unravel."

"Do you honestly think that it's that serious?" pressed Mark.

"Please go there, Mark. It's the way he was talking. Whatever this is, I think it's big. I have to call the agent back within two hours, and I need to warn Rebecca. I want to be able to tell her that you'll be there with her."

"Wilson certainly has you spooked. OK, I'll reschedule my appointment and head to the cabin. I'll call you once I'm there.

"Thanks so much, Mark. "I owe you."

"You'll owe me alright. But try not to worry. I'll be with her shortly to handle things."

John hung up and immediately called his wife.

"You always told me not to talk while driving," she complained. "I'm on I-85, and the traffic is lousy. What is it"

"This is important. Agent Wilson of the FBI says that they've found additional information about the man murdered in the mountains. He intends to question you at the cabin this afternoon."

"What?"

"Mark is headed your way and should be there before the FBI agent arrives. Wilson refused to go into details, but said that it couldn't wait until you were back in Atlanta."

"What do you..."

Suddenly, John heard a loud sound and then the screech of tires against the pavement. There was a series of tremendously loud noises, and then silence.

"Rebecca!" he called out. "Are you all right? Rebecca!"

Silence.

Chapter 36
Pie

"**You need to** see about Grady," Mark said, attempting to pull his friend away from Rebecca's lifeless body.

"It's cold in this place," John said, pulling the sheet closer around his deceased wife's neck.

"Grady," repeated Mark. "You've been standing in this morgue for two hours. You should see about Grady."

"It still doesn't seem real. I can't just leave her here. I don't know any of these people."

"We'll take good care of her, Mr. Walker," said the owner of a funeral home in Jackson County, Georgia. "I promise that we won't do anything until your approval is granted."

John nodded his head. The man slowly closed the mortuary cabinet, causing her body to be out of sight.

"Grady," whispered Mark.

"You're right," John said. "Is he still with Jody?"

"She offered to have him stay the night with her, depending on your wishes," explained Mark.

"I don't know what to say to him. When I left him with her, I told Grady that his mother had an accident in her car. I have to tell him; I just don't know how."

As the two exited the building, the setting sun cast a red glow on the surroundings.

"Grady's so smart," John said. "It was unfair to leave him with Jody. I've left her to answer all his questions, and he'll not take any BS from anyone. I'm sure she's having a difficult time."

"He's in good hands," replied Mark. "You couldn't bring him here."

John glanced back over his shoulder at the rural funeral home, before opening the front passenger door of Mark's car.

"Maybe you should give her a ring," suggested Mark, as his car pulled from the parking lot.

"I feel totally exhausted, but you're right," said John. "I don't understand how the front wheel of that car could come off. I've kept it maintained regularly."

"I have no idea. What did the state trooper say?"

"There were witnesses driving on I-85. Several provided statements. The front passenger wheel came off the car, and that she immediately lost control. The car left the road, flipped several times, before striking a large tree."

"I can't imagine."

"It seems consistent with what I heard on my cell. It all happened really fast."

"Has the state opened an investigation?" asked Mark.

"Just a preliminary one," answered John. "An expert will conduct a thorough investigation within the week. The car struck the tree in the same area as the missing wheel, and the damage is severe."

"Let me know what I can do to help. If your insurance company gives you trouble, I'd be glad to step in."

"Thanks," sighed John.

"It's a miracle that she didn't have Grady with her."

"She didn't want him in the paint – Grady! I need to make that call to Jody. Oh, God, I can't imagine what he's dealing with. He's so smart – he has to know that something is wrong."

John quickly punched in Jody's number.

"Jody, Mark and I are on our way back to Atlanta. How is Grady?"

"I've tried to keep him busy, but his questions haven't ceased," replied Jody. "I told him that he'll have to ask you, that you're on the scene, and that you have the information."

"Thank you, so much," replied John. He could hear his three-year-old son in the background requesting the phone.

"Put him on," said John.

Jody handed it to the little man.

"Daddy, Mama got hurt bad, didn't she?" the small voice questioned.

"Yes, she did," he answered. "I'm on my way home, and I'll tell you all about it when I get there. I'll be with you really soon. Have you been good for Jody?"

"Did Mama die?" Grady asked.

"Oh, little Buddy," John's voice choked.

— • ● • —

Grady stood as tall as he could in his little suit, watching people file into the rural church. John led him to the front pew and seated him between himself and Mark Fairchild. Mark tapped him on his small thigh. Turning, Grady saw Mark pull a lollipop from his coat.

"Thank you," Grady whispered, before popping it in his mouth.

Within a few moments, Pastor Bill Whitworth stood behind the pulpit. Grady had sobbed, on and off, for three days, but that morning he seemed to be remarkably at peace. He removed the lollipop and held it in his small right hand as Rebecca's favorite hymn was sung. Grady immediately placed it back in his mouth when the song was over.

Words from the minister seemed to pour over John's aching soul. Grady listened close, as he talked about heaven and how happy Rebecca must be there.

"In John's gospel, chapter fourteen tells us about heaven," Bill Whitworth said, slipping on a pair of glasses. "Do not let your hearts be troubled. You believe in God; believe also in me. My Father's house has many rooms; if that were not so, would I have told you that I am going there to prepare a place for you? And if I go and prepare a place for you, I will come back and take you to be with me that you also may be where I am."

Removing the glasses, Bill's eyes locked on Grady's. He paused a few seconds before continuing.

"Rebecca's life on this earth has ended. But as her last breath left her body, Jesus took her in His arms and carried her to be with Him in a place that is too incredible for us to truly imagine. Those of us living can't see that place with our physical human eyes. Only the spiritual eyes of the dead are able to see it. There are so many distractions here on this earth, which divert our attention to focus on everything else. There, she has no more pain, no more sadness, no more worry – forever. Those spiritual eyes of Rebecca are no longer consumed with all those issues presented to her while she was living on earth. There, she now sees Heaven as it really is and she completely senses the love of God. It's unlike anything we could imagine. The world is a dangerous place, but there she is completely safe. Jesus is the very best at taking care of someone. God has appointed times for each of us to go and be with her, but until then we are to live the best lives possible here on earth. God has so much for us all. There is no telling what we will find along the way in life, and we should continually look for His works in all that we experience."

The minister stepped out from behind the pulpit, to the center of the platform. He addressed those attending.

"There will be a private and brief graveside ceremony shortly at the cemetery of St. Paul Methodist Church, not far from John's cabin. Go in peace."

John had selected six men to escort the casket back to the hearse waiting outside. Rebecca's body was loaded, while people exited the church. As John led Grady down the steps of the church, he focused on his son.

"Where did you get that sucker?" John asked.

Grady's small finger pointed to Mark.

"Guilty, as charged," Mark admitted.

The hearse was accompanied by a handful of private vehicles to the gravesite. John had her buried beside the grave of Lilly Johnson in the small church cemetery. After prayers were made, John thanked Bill for his services and handed him an envelope containing a check for a thousand dollars. The Minister gave John a last bit of consolation, and then left.

"I plan to meet with you to make a few changes in my will," John said to Mark.

"Anytime, friend," Mark answered.

"Can I come?" asked Grady.

"Sure," answered John.

"That's an interesting headstone," Mark observed. "I've never seen one with a deep square recess carved in it."

"There was only this single plot available in that area of the cemetery that Rebecca cherished, so I ordered a special tombstone for her that contains a boxed area which will hold a small vase for my ashes when I die," explained John. An engraved copper plate will seal it."

"You plan to be cremated?" Mark asked.

Before John could answer, a small voice interrupted.

"Is anybody hungry for lunch," Grady asked.

"This morning, you couldn't eat breakfast," John replied.

"Now that I know that Mama's safe, I'm hungry," said Grady. "I want a burger at Sally's."

"I think that sounds really good," said John.

"Mark has to come," demanded Grady.

"OK, said Mark.

"Daddy, I want you to buy Mark a piece of Sally's cheery pie," said Grady.

"Mark, are you up for cherry pie?" asked John. "Grady calls it cheery pie."

"If Grady is giving the endorsement, it has to be

good," Mark replied. "Sure."

Grady glanced up at his father with a grin.

"But it would be best for you to buy all three of us cheery pie," suggested Grady. "I don't want Mark to have to eat it all alone."

For the first time in days, John smiled.

"It's a deal," he replied to his son.

"Who taught him to triangulate, like that?" asked Mark. "The kid's only three!"

258

Chapter 37
Revelations

"**Mr. Walker, I'm** sorry for the loss of your wife," began agent Wilson.

"Thank you," replied John.

"I came to your condo to inform you of recently obtained information relating to the man found dead in the mountains."

"I really can't see how this matters anymore. But go ahead and say what you want to say."

"Through forensics, we've finally identified that man as Charles Everett. Because of the DNA match between him and your wife, we believe your wife to really be his daughter Jessica Everett from Anson County, North Carolina."

"Oh, come on!" exclaimed John. "You believe? Do you have evidence to this being fact?"

"The DNA evidence is pretty strong," answered the agent. "It's my duty to share this evidence with you."

"Knock yourself out," said John.

"Mr. Everett left his wife Debbie when she was pregnant with his daughter Jessica and moved to be with a communal group in the mountains of northeast Georgia. Records from Jessica's high school showed her to be a brilliant student, but she dropped out her senior year. Pictures of Jessica in the school yearbook have some resemblance to your wife. But the appearance of teens can change substantially over a following decade. So, there is nothing conclusive in these photos."

"Then, why are you here?" asked John.

"Please hear me out, Mr. Walker. Debbie Everett was an alcoholic, and eventually died from liver damage. It's possible it was a miserable environment for the daughter. We believe that, at some point, Debbie Everett told her daughter the general location of the commune joined by Mr. Everett. We know that Jessica left home before graduating, and for eight years worked odd jobs in small towns across North Carolina before setting out for the mountains of northeast Georgia."

"I should have counted every time you used the word 'believe', as opposed to the one instance where you used the word 'know'. What do you want from me?"

"I told you the truth when I stated my purpose for being here," said agent Wilson. "We're not demanding anything of you. When we first contacted you, prior to your wife's death, we absolutely wanted to press her for further investigation. But now it may be pointless."

"You've done that, and you're free to go any time," said John.

"Please bear with me a little longer, Mr. Walker."

"Please get to the point."

"Mr. Everett had no son by Jessica's mother, so we have no reason to continue our search for the man that your wife claimed to be her brother. We're putting that aspect to bed. The purpose of my visit here today, is to tell you that the case has now been made inactive."

"I'm glad to hear that," stated John. "Are you closing this case, stating that my wife, Rebecca Johnson, was really this Jessica Everett? If so, you can BELIEVE whatever you wish, but I am not changing the name on my wife's tombstone. And if a name change is the real purpose of this visit, we can end this and I'll immediately contact my lawyer."

"We don't have the conclusive evidence proving that to be the case, we can only conjecture about the identity," said Wilson. "Based on employee records and interviews, we believe that Jessica Everett set off to find her birth father. That she researched the surrounding area of northeast Georgia and studied the history of it to better know it. In our search of anyone named Rebecca Johnson, we were shocked to find an old photo of a woman by that name who had a remarkable resemblance of your wife. We think she ran across the story of Grady and Rebecca Johnson of the 1920s, saw her likeness in this photo of Rebecca, and read about how the woman disappeared. At some point, we believe she decided to take on the identity of Rebecca Johnson. About a year before your wife appeared out of nowhere claiming to be Rebecca Johnson, Jessica Everett totally disappeared off the radar. Your effort to establish your wife's US citizenship as Rebecca Johnson, fixed that as her legal name. But that didn't change the fact that she may really be Jessica Everett, who we believe came to this area in search of her father."

"So, does this mean that your files indicate that the FBI believes my wife killed those two people in the mountains? Is this what you're saying?"

"We suspect it's highly possible, but most of what we have is circumstantial. We have no hard evidence showing that she ever found her father. If your wife was still alive, we would press her about the story she provided. We no longer believe it to be the truth. Perjury is a crime. But you're correct. Now that your wife is dead, there's really nothing left for us to pursue regarding her. We've concluded that your wife possibly killed them, but we determined the case should be made inactive due to lack of evidence."

"This is what you wanted to let me know?" asked John.

"That's it."

"If you ever make your CONCLUSION public, I will have my attorney all over you," warned John. "I have a son, who doesn't need to have additional pain in his life. If you bring this back by publicizing any of the garbage, I will sue the living crap out of you people. Do you understand me?"

"I was sincere, when I told you that I'm very sorry for your loss," added the agent. "I don't anticipate any publicity over this, because of the lack of hard evidence. In all of our investigations, we've found you to be remarkably clean for a man of your means. Whatever the truth, your wife seemed to be a wonderful mother to your son. I am truly sorry for what this family is enduring. Mr. Walker, if there is anything that I can do for you and your son, please let me know."

"It would be great to know if the FBI had ideas about how a meticulously maintained car can simply loose a front wheel when traveling down a highway," replied John. "It makes no sense to me. It was a well-built car."

"I wouldn't know," said Wilson. "I'd like to ask you another question. Did your wife ever indicate that she had made enemies in the past?"

"No."

"Even under the name Jessica Everett?" the agent asked.

"No. Please stop with the name thing. So, is the FBI interested in investigating the accident?"

"I'm afraid that the FBI doesn't have jurisdiction to be involved. That investigation would be the job of the state of Georgia."

"Thanks, anyway."

"Do you suspect foul play?" asked the agent.

"I honestly don't know what to think."

—•●•—

Ten days after the visit by agent Wilson, John received a call from the Georgia State Patrol investigator who was looking into Rebecca's accident.

"Mr. Walker, my name is Sam Fielding, an investigator for the state. After a thorough investigation of your wife's accident, I believe there is a strong possibility that someone tampered with the car she was driving."

"What?" exclaimed John.

"I would like for you come by our office," continued the investigator. "I'd like to show you that evidence and ask you a few questions. "I'm on my way," replied John. "I plan to bring my attorney."

"I'm not sure that an attorney is needed," stated investigator Fielding.

"I want a second pair of eyes and a sharp mind."

"That will be fine."

Grabbing his keys, John quickly placed a call to Mark Fairchild.

"Mark, the state investigator believes that Rebecca's car was tampered with. I'm on my way to their office to review evidence, and I would really appreciate some company."

"I can wrap up a few things within a half hour," replied Mark. "Do you want to pick me up?"

"Absolutely. I'm going to notify Grady's daycare that I will probably be late picking him up. I'll head your way."

Chapter 38
Evidence

"**Man, you need** to slow down," said Mark. "We're on our way to the Georgia State Patrol office!"

"Maybe so," agreed John.

"I can see us going airborne into the parking lot of that place," said Mark.

"This is important."

"It's also important that we don't get killed or arrested."

"Agreed," said John.

He dropped the SUV into cruise control, at three miles per hour over the speed limit. John turned to Mark.

"Better?"

"Better," replied Mark.

Arriving at the state office, John informed the receptionist that Sam Fielding was expecting his visit. He and Mark were escorted to a small conference room by a female officer. Mark took a small notepad from his coat pocket.

"Investigator Fielding should join you shortly," said the escorting officer. "Would either of you want something to drink? Maybe a cup of coffee?"

"Please," answered John. "We both take it black."

Immediately after the female officer delivered the coffee, Sam Fielding entered the room. The investigator's clear blue eyes flashed at her.

"I'll take one too," the large man said.

John estimated him to he at least six feet four inches, with thick powerful hands. His graying hair was cut short.

"Right away," replied the female trooper.

Mark nudged John and scribbled a note on his pad.

A bit sexist, don't you think?

John nodded, as Mark flipped to a new sheet.

"Sam Fielding," the large man stated, extending a hand toward John.

"Good to meet you," replied John. "My attorney, Mark Fairchild."

"Mr. Fairchild," said Fielding, with a nod.

"You said that you suspect my wife's car was tampered with," said John.

"I do," Fielding replied, pulling several large photos from a manila folder. He slid the photos across the table to John.

"If you'll take a look at these," continued the investigator. "I have several shots that I want you to see."

The female officer entered the room and handed Fielding the cup of coffee.

"We conducted a forensic investigation using a SEM, Scanning Electron Microscope," explained Fielding. "It provides high resolution surface imaging. We've found tool markings on two lugs of the wheel."

"Tool markings?" asked John. "These lugs were cut almost half in two."

"We see this type of pattern when a hacksaw has been used," replied Fielding.

"I want this son of a bitch caught!" blurted John. His eyes were filled with rage.

"I do too," replied Fielding, his eyes bore a hole through John.

"Wait!" blurted John. "You think that I had something to do with this?"

"I don't know who used the hacksaw on the lugs," answered Fielding. "You insisted that your lawyer be present with you at this meeting. Could be anybody, could be you."

"I didn't come here as his lawyer; I'm his friend," stated Mark. "However, if you think John Walker wanted his wife killed, you are absolutely mistaken. I can certainly turn on the attorney switch, and this meeting will take on a much different tone. Is he being investigated?"

"Everyone is being investigated until I know more," answered Fielding.

There was a knock at the door, and it opened. The female trooper handed Fielding a report. He looked it over in silence.

"Why would a man of your means have such a puny life insurance policy on his wife?" Fielding asked John. "Seems like you have only the minimal accidental death insurance allowed on your automobile insurance. Nothing more. I see that you have no other policy."

"Because I HAVE money!" shouted John. "I don't need to have a fat policy to bury my wife. I can simply pay for it."

"Calm down, John," advised Mark. "When the police suspect that a murder of a married woman has been committed, they first look at the husband. This is standard procedure.”

“Most husbands who kill their wives do it for either money, hate, or the guy wants his wife gone because he’s hot for another woman,” Fielding said to John. “In your case, I can pretty much rule out the money aspect.”

“Thanks a lot,” said John, sarcastically.

“I’ve known John for more than fifteen years, and I’ve known his wife for about five,” said Mark. “I’ve never seen a couple more in love. Believe me, John Walker is stupid in love with his wife. She has absolutely turned him into a puppy. They have a son, Grady. I’ve never witnessed such a stable family. If you’re seriously looking at John Walker, you’re barking up the wrong tree. You need to find out who did this, and you are totally wasting time on this man.”

“So, who else?” asked Fielding, turning his attention on John. “Who would want her dead?”

“I have no idea,” answered John. “If you find him, I’d like to get my hands on him.”

“You keep saying, ‘him” – why do you think a man did this?” asked Fielding. “How about a woman?”

“I have no idea who would want to hurt her,” said John.

“We picked up the FBI records on her,” said Fielding. “I had a chat with agent Wilson. Did you already suspect something?”

“No,” answered John. “Not a clue. Wait, did the FBI make those records public?”

“No,” answered Fielding. “The GCIC, or Georgia Crime Information Center, can access FBI records through a network known as the Criminal Justice

Information System. The CJIS serves as a communications system for local law enforcement. access to the FBI's National Crime Information Center (NCIC) files. Various records are linked."

"John, what is he talking about?" asked Mark.

"We can talk about it later," said John. "I promise."

"Well, it certainly complicates things," said Fielding. "Don't you agree?"

"My wife is dead," said John. "My son's mother is dead. I just want this person, man or woman, caught."

"This is all for now," stated Fielding. "I'm on this, like stink on a turd, Mr. Walker. I'll contact you whenever I find anything."

"Thank you," said Mark. "You'll be talking to both of us."

John and Mark were escorted from the building. In the parking lot, Mark turned to his friend.

"What is going on with the FBI?"

"Let's get in the car," answered John. "I'll explain everything."

John told him about agent Wilson's visit, and of their belief that his wife was really Jessica Everett. He asked Mark to swear that he would keep that information private between the two of them.

"Wow!" exclaimed Mark. "Talking about a bombshell. So, Rebecca is really this Jessica Everett?"

"Hold on," answered John. "They have no proof of that."

"You wife's DNA showed that she was related to the man murdered in the mountains, who has now been identified as Charles Everett, whose missing daughter is Jessica Everett," said Mark. "This Everett girl goes missing about a year before your future wife drops out of the woods from nowhere with no ID. Using a wild story, she convinces you to help her establish her identification as Rebecca Johnson. Am I missing something?"

"Well, that's pretty much how agent Wilson laid it out."

"Does the FBI believe that this Jessica Everett made enemies in the past?" asked Mark. "Years before. Do you think they believe an enemy of hers killed her?"

"My wife's name is Rebecca, not Jessica!" shouted John. "Got it?"

"OK, OK. I was just thinking …"

"Stop with that, please," begged John.

"I mean, it all makes sense now," said Mark.

"What makes sense?"

"She was always so secretive about her past. Once she began talking about it, her stories were everywhere. She lived in a commune in the mountains since she was born. No, she was really transported through time from the 1920s. The things she came up with were completely bizarre. I tried to warn you about her, and I was right. Now, all of this makes sense. Good Lord! How are you handling this? I would be a basket case."

"As far as I'm concerned, she was Rebecca Johnson," answered John. "I loved her like I've loved no one else, and I'll continue to love her. She's the mother of my only son, Grady. That will never change."

"Grady. Grady certainly doesn't need this kind of instability in his life. He's been through too much already. I'm astounded."

"At what?" asked John.

"I'm astounded at you. I've never in my life

witnessed a man with your inner strength. At this kind of news, I'd be broken up like crackers smashed by a sledgehammer. But, not you. You desperately want to know who meddled with that wheel, but otherwise you're as calm as ever. Nothing rattles you."

"If you think about it, you'll remember times when I was pretty rattled," replied John. "Do you remember how I was when she moved out?"

"I do. But once you two finally settled on your feelings about each other, you've been like a rock. You were concerned about the early investigation by the FBI. But that concern wasn't about yourself, it was about the welfare of your wife."

"Rebecca," said John. "You can use her name, Rebecca."

"OK. Rebecca."

"I'm trusting you with this," stated John. "We are talking about the stability of Grady's life. Nothing has changed. His mother was Rebecca Johnson."

"I won't slip up," replied Mark. "You can trust me."

"I'm focused on two things," said John, his eyes blazed. "I'm focused on who wanted Rebecca harmed, and I'm focused on the safety of my son Grady. I need to find the person who tampered with those lugs, and I'm going to need our friendship to be unshakeable."

"It is," Mark stated. "You don't have to worry about that."

272

Chapter 39
Oath

"**Rebecca really liked** you," John told Larry Taylor.

"Your wife was someone special," replied Larry. "She was gold."

"Grady really likes you, too."

John's son would do something silly, and the huge man's entire body would shake with laughter. Grady loved him. John had mentioned more than once to Danny about how well Larry and Grady hit it off. Larry had periodically been assigned to John by Danny as somewhat of a babysitter for Grady, whenever interviews by the state investigator ran over the scheduled times. It was Danny's idea.

"I don't expect more interviews this week," said John. "I'm sure there are things with which you would rather occupy your time."

"That little man of yours is great," replied Larry. "The kid's brilliant, but there's nothing nerdy about him. He has soul like I've never seen in a child. It's like he can sense things about me — what occupies my thoughts, and how I'm feeling on a particular day. How does he do that? He's not quite four years old."

"He likes you a lot. He tells me about your stories and the games you two play."

"I told you that I would be honest with you," said Larry. "It's Danny. He is constantly babbling about some papers in your possession. I thought he would drop it."

"Has he indicated what concerns he has about these papers?" asked John.

"I have no idea," answered Larry.

"Rebecca didn't like Danny," said John. "I could never convince her that he was a loyal family friend; that he is more than just an employee."

"I think your wife made that clear to Danny. I believe the feeling was mutual. He's never had anything positive to say about her. Danny told me once that she never paid him any respect, and that she had threatened him on one occasion."

"Threatened him? What about?"

"Beats me. Who knows? You know, some people just don't like each other. Like it's something chemical, or something. It's like nature has built them to butt heads. Like when you place two magnets of the same polarity together. They're going to push apart. Toleration is the best they can do. Maybe it was something like that."

"That's a pretty good analogy, Larry" observed John. "You hear people talking about polar opposites, but it's the same polarity that really drives magnets apart. That's an astute observation. No wonder Grady likes you so much. I've seen rough men in biker bars give way to your leadership because of your physical stature. Like a pack of dogs standing down around the leader of the pack. But under all that, you're a thinker."

"I'm not sure what to think about that, Mr. Walker," replied Larry. "In one sense you're telling me that I have a fair head on my shoulders, but then you tell me that I'm like a wild dog."

"First of all, you can drop the Mr. Walker bit," said John. "We've known each other long enough for you to call me John. Secondly, there is nothing negative in what I said. A different way of putting it is that physically you're a natural leader who also thinks things through."

"I'd like to go with the second way you put it. I appreciate that, JOHN."

"There you go; call me by my name," John said, with a chuckle.

"Since we're being honest, why would someone of your means and prominence in the business world want to be on first name basis with someone like me?" asked Larry.

"Rebecca was a really good judge of character," answered John. "She thought very highly of you, and I would trust that over the most impressive resume ever handed to me. I trusted her."

"Thank you."

"What else has Danny said about these papers?" asked John.

"It's like they're eating at him. I'm guessing that they have something to do with the past, something he would like left alone. He once said that digging up the past was like digging up a dead body. That some things just need to be left alone."

"A dead body? Like that dead body found in the wall of that building I was having remodeled?"

"I'm not saying that!" exclaimed Larry. "I don't know anything about that."

"Listen, I've known Danny all my life. But this

animosity between him and Rebecca concerns me a little."

"I don't like it, either."

"How would you feel about pushing his buttons a little?" asked John.

"You want me to get a rise out of him?"

"I want you to talk up Rebecca every time that you see him. If he becomes agitated, keep pushing."

"He's liable to fire me."

"If he does, then you'll work directly for me," said John. "I have plenty of things I could pay you to do."

—•●•—

Two weeks later, Larry and John met in secret at a diner in South Carolina. John could see the rage the big man carried by the way he walked into the place. They sat at a booth farthest from the register and away from windows. It was apparent to John that even the waitress sensed the anger. She appeared somewhat apprehensive when she took Larry's order. As she walked away, Larry spoke.

"Danny's worse than a turd. Crap has some redeeming value; it can be used for fertilizer."

"What happened?" asked John.

"At first, he screamed his head off at me every time I laid it on thick about Rebecca. Then he got nasty – and personal. He accused her of sucking me off whenever I came around your place when you weren't there. I wanted to pop his ugly head off."

"Really?"

"At one point, he threw a tire tool across a garage

and cursed her. He said that he was glad that the 'bitch' was dead, that maybe life would get back to normal."

"Seriously?"

"That man has a nasty side that I don't think you've ever known about," said Larry. "I wouldn't put it past him to have tampered with her car."

"What makes you say that?" asked John.

"You know there's an old saying. A hit dog hollers. He did a lot of hollering. I've known killers. When I pressed him harder about how much I thought of her, he had the stone-cold eyes of a killer. I'm telling you, he's glad that she is dead."

"Thanks," said John. "I'll take it from here."

———•●•———

The following week, John met with Danny about the possibilities of expanding his services.

"I have to ask your opinion about something," John said.

"Sure," replied Danny.

"My parents saved their most important items in a safe, and I'm a little confused about a set of papers. They have to do with the remodeling they had done years ago on that building containing that dead body. Why would they have thought those papers were special?"

Danny's eyes narrowed.

"You're a smart man, John," Danny said. "I would think those papers would contain names of people associated with that old remodeling. I think you have your own ideas about why those papers are important."

"You mean, like the fact that you and your services were in charge of twenty-four-seven surveillance of the building during the remodeling, most likely during the time when that body was placed in that wall."

"I would like to see those papers," said Danny. "If they deal with security, then maybe I should have them for safe keeping."

"You didn't like Rebecca much, did you?"

"She's dead. She's got nothing to do with our current conversation."

"She's got plenty to do with it," said John, stepping close to Danny. "She saw those papers, and she told me that she believed my folks held those papers over you to ensure your loyalty. She told me that she thought you were rotten. Rebecca couldn't stand you, and I know for a fact that you felt the same way about her."

"I took a lot of shit from your folks, but I wasn't about to take it from that woman," blurted Danny.

His countenance changed from that of being a compassionate Godfather of the man he was speaking with, to the stone-cold killer Larry had seen. Four inches shorter than John, his eyes seemed to climb up to the same level of John's. For the first time in his life, John saw the soul of the man he had once called Uncle Danny in those eyes. They spewed hate.

"Cool it!" ordered John.

"You cool it!" barked Danny. "Don't ever forget that I'm what stands between you and the worst the world can offer. I've given you protection your entire life. I'm your Godfather, you ungrateful twit. I swore an oath. Your life could be snuffed out in a heartbeat, not to mention that little kid of yours. You get me?"

"Loud and clear," answered John. "That oath was to my parents and me, and not my wife. Isn't that right?"

"You don't seem to understand what an oath to God means," said Danny. "The words matter. God holds me to those words, and nothing outside those words."

"Oath to God - is that why you're so faithful about attending mass?" asked John. "Do you think that as long as you are faithful to a vow before God, that you can just go to confession about all the other horrible things you might want to do – and everything is just cozy with God?"

"I swore an oath to GOD regarding your parents, and all of their bloodline," explained Danny. "Unless you force my hand to abandon that oath, I would never turn away from you and your son. You should have never allowed your wife near those papers. You failed her; not that she didn't deserve what she got. You…"

John grabbed Danny by his collar and slammed him up against a wall. He suddenly felt a kinship of hate with this man. A cold chill ran down his back. He remembered Grady, and then remembered himself. He lowered Danny to the floor, released him, and walked away.

Chapter 40
Safety

"**Grady should be** safe," John told Larry. "Danny let me know that Grady and I would be safe long as I never force his hand."

"How could you be sure about that?" asked Larry. "What exactly does that mean?"

"Danny swore an oath to God."

Larry exploded into laughter.

"No, he's serious about it," John said, trying to bring the conversation back in line."

"No way, man!" Larry spouted out, as he began to get hold of himself. "Don't tell me that he convinced you that he's a religious man."

"It's certainly nothing like my faith, but he has his own thing about God and oaths."

"Your faith?" asked Larry.

"I'm trying. Before I met Rebecca, faith in God was the farthest thing from my mind. But her faith was really strong. I saw something in her, and I want it to still be there for Grady."

"I think I understand," said Larry, now serious. "That's a good thing, it really is."

"Danny, on the other hand, sees things much differently than I do. He's Catholic, but not like any

Catholic I've ever known. He's feels bound to this oath to God, and he can't allow himself to fail it in any way. For everything else, he believes he can just go to the priest for forgiveness. It's actually pretty simple. Hang on to the oath, and just have the priest cleanse him of anything else – no matter how horrible it is. It's more like a superstition than what I would call a faith."

"That priest has probably gone deaf from listening to his confessions," said Larry. "Oath or no oath, that man is evil."

"According to him, his oath ensures protection for Grady and me. I'm really torn on this. I wanted to break his neck. I'm all but certain that he was the person who tampered with Rebecca's car. On the other hand, I want to make sure that Grady's safe."

"He admitted the tampering, or is this just a hunch of yours?"

"He let me know that the protection was only for people in my parent's bloodline, me and Grady."

"But not Rebecca?"

"Not Rebecca. He can't stand her."

"I don't get you!" yelled Larry. "If I thought that, and Rebecca was my wife, I would beat him senseless before breaking his neck. I know that you aren't like that. Why don't you give those papers to the law? Turn him over and let them put him away. He's old. He's bound to die in prison."

"People who control others outside of prison, often find ways to have their bidding done while behind bars," explained John. "He pretty much let me know that the only thing that ensures the safety of Grady and myself, is the fact that I've not yet pushed him to ignore his oath. If I put him in prison, that oath wouldn't mean crap to him. In his mind, I would have forced him to abandon it. I think he would have us both killed."

"So, there are conditions on him keeping his oath to God?" asked Larry. "What kind of crap oath is that?"

"It's all in his mind, his weird standards."

"What does he want from you?" asked Larry. "He didn't confess this to you for no reason."

"What do you mean?"

"He confessed the oath, and that you could force his hand to abandon it. What does he want from you that will ensure your loyalty to him? What does he want in exchange for maintaining his oath?"

"I think you're right," answered John. "Until now, I didn't fully understand what he was saying."

"What does he want?"

"He wants some paperwork that I have stored in a safe place."

"What kind of paperwork?" asked Larry.

"It's just some paperwork that my parents held over him," answered John.

"If he has this paperwork, do you really think that you and Grady are safe? Stop and think about it. Was his oath good enough for your parents? No. That's why they held this paperwork over his head. They didn't trust him, and neither should you."

"You're right," agreed John. "I can't let him have that paperwork."

"You didn't tell him where the documents are held, did you?" asked Larry. "Tell me that you didn't let that information slip out."

"I let him know that they are in a safe."

"You need to get Grady to a safe place," advised Larry. "Every time I was at the cabin, he prodded me about those papers. He suspected that you had them near the cabin, and you just let him know that they reside in a safe. If you don't give them to him soon, he won't hesitate to send in a team to find that safe in that cabin. Once he has those documents, you and Grady are toast."

"Oh, my Lord!" exclaimed John.

"I want you to leave with Grady right now," advised Larry. "I want you to trust me to handle this. I'll call you if I believe you and Grady are actually safe."

— • ● • —

Two days later, a news reporter told Atlanta that a security service owner named Danny Moffato was found dead on a sidewalk in the rear of a ten-story building which was under construction. His hands had been bound with a zip-tie, and the police believe that he had been thrown from the roof of the building.

"I can't believe that your head of security was murdered," said Mark, on a call to John.

"Yeah, what a shock," John replied.

"Head of your security," said Mark. "How secure do you feel right now? We're not talking about one of his guys, we are talking about Danny Moffato. That can't be a source of comfort to you."

"Actually, I haven't felt more comfortable in a long time," said John. "I don't know, it's hard to explain."

"So, what are you doing for security? Danny has been there your entire life."

"I'm in the process of purchasing the security

company, and I plan to put Larry Taylor in charge," stated John. "Same service, but a different manager."

"Larry Taylor?" blurted Mark. "You plan to put that oaf in charge of your security firm?"

"I've gotten to know him, Mark. Larry Taylor is no oaf. You'd be surprised."

"I don't know."

"I trust him," said John. "I trust him with my life."

"And   Grady's?"

"Especially, Grady's. Hey, Larry and Minister Whitworth are coming out to the cabin to do a little fishing weekend after next. Why don't you come out and join us?"

"I think I will," answered Mark.

"Grady would love that," replied John. "Bill Whitworth is astounded by Grady's intelligence, and the two of them get into elementary discussions about philosophy and religion. I think Grady views him as a type of grandfather role. I hope you'll come. Maybe we'll get some of Sally Perkin's cherry pie."

"OK, I'm sold on the cherry pie," said Mark. "I really don't know the minister very well. You seem to think that he's good for Grady."

"I once asked Bill Whitworth if he knew the percentage of a person's life which was totally an act of God – I'm talking about what percentage was due to nature and the laws of the universe, and what percentage was determined by our own decisions and acts."

"What did he say?" asked Mark.

"He said that he would love to have those answers, but that he simply didn't know," answered John. "That's when I began to like the man. He isn't pompous, and he doesn't act as if he is all knowing about God. Bill is refreshingly honest."

"I'm glad Grady has good role models in his life," said Mark. "Your son is incredibly intelligent for his age."

"Grady thinks Bobby Thompson, the guy who delivers our firewood, is dumb."

Mark chuckled.

Chapter 41
Genius

"Mark, Grady's first grade teacher suggested that I have his intelligence tested," said John. "Rebecca wanted to have him evaluated when he was three to see if he was gifted. This is an IQ test. I didn't even know that the IQs of six-year-olds were tested, but I gave permission for the test."

"He's smart," replied Mark. "Everybody knows that. He began reading at three. It doesn't surprise me that she recommended testing him."

"His teacher told me that he continually asks her for more advanced reading material," said John. "She began bringing him books for higher grade levels. Grady shows an incredible aptitude for study. He has been in elementary school for only six weeks, and he's completed all of the material meant for the fifth grade."

"You've got to be kidding me!" exclaimed Mark. "So, did you have him tested?"

"The results showed him to have in IQ of 168," answered John. "Grady's a genius, for real. Both his teacher and the principal of the school believe that he should be placed in a school for the gifted, so that he can study at his own pace."

"Have you found a school?"

"There are several in the Atlanta area, and I plan to have him visit a few," answered John. "My son, a genius. This is nuts! I knew he was really smart."

"Maybe he needs a private school," suggested Mark.

"The testing center provided a list of recommended schools, but I'm pretty much in the dark about which would be best for Grady.

Grady finished high school at the age of ten. Several colleges and universities were interested in giving him scholarships, but John questioned Grady's emotional maturity regarding being placed in a college environment.

"Is there a particular area of study that you'd like to pursue?" John asked Grady.

"Bioengineering sounds interesting," Grady answered. "But no, I'm not really sure. I also find the field of genetics to be fascinating."

"So, you're leaning toward a medical field?"

"Maybe it would be best to enter as a pre-med student, and go from there," replied Grady. "I know that you're busy, but I think that I would like to commute the first year. I don't like the idea of being separated from you at my age."

"I would love to do that. I believe that's a sound idea."

"I love it here at the cabin and know you do as well. The University of Georgia is about an hour and half away. That's a long commute. If I decided to attend

Georgia Tech or Georgia State, it would mean moving to Atlanta on a more permanent basis. I'm still not sure which scholarship would be best."

"There's no rush. Take your time. I'll support whatever you want."

"Dad, I'd like to ask you a few questions regarding my mother," stated Grady.

"Fire away," said John.

"Why did you select that cemetery of that tiny church as the place to bury her?" Grady asked. "Neither of you attended that church. I know that it's close to the cabin, but I think there must have been some significance in that particular cemetery."

John released a deep sigh. He rose from his chair, opened the safe, and removed an envelope from it. He slid the envelope into the inner pocket of his jacket.

"Why don't we place flowers on your mother's grave?" suggested John. "Maybe we can talk about it there."

"I would like that," replied Grady.

Grady and his father picked several flowers from a bed near the cabin and placed them in a vase. The ten-year-old dutifully held the vase as John drove them to the small cemetery. Once there, Grady placed the vase of flowers at the base of Rebecca's tombstone.

"Tell me," Grady requested.

John took the envelope from his pocket, removed the contents, and handed them to Grady. The genius boy read over the information and handed the paperwork back to his father.

"Now, tell me the significance of what I just read," Grady said.

The following discussion lasted close to an hour.

Grady soaked in every word uttered by his father. Questions from Grady were met with ready answers from John.

"I'm glad that they didn't try to force you to change the name on the tombstone to Everett," said Grady.

"Your mother's official name was Rebecca Walker," said John. "A name change wasn't going to happen, no matter what the FBI or the state of Georgia had attempted to do. Mark and I wouldn't have allowed it."

"I've always liked Mark. I'm glad you have a best friend of your age. I've really never known that kind of relationship. I've always been more comfortable with older people. Do you think that I should have made a greater effort with kids of my age?"

"I know that it's been difficult," answered John. "The way I look at it is, that you have an adult mind riding around inside a ten-year-old body. That's extremely unusual. There just aren't many others of your physical age who are experiencing the same situation. I suspect that you've been a little lonely."

"Not really," said Grady. "I think that a person may not be able to really miss what he's never experienced."

"Were there any kids in your school for the gifted who you counted as friends?" asked John.

"I believe they were more like acquaintances, than real friends." answered Grady. "I don't know why so many exceptionally brilliant kids have to be arrogant with others."

"So, some of them can be jerks?" asked John.

"Jerks would be a kind way of putting it,"

answered Grady. "They would try to talk to me behind the backs of others, and what they had to say was so ugly that it caused me to question their intelligence. But I never said that to them."

"Question their intelligence?" asked John.

"The way I see it is that people work with what they've been given. I'm not an athlete, but I've never been made to feel athletically inferior by those who are. I was born with a gifted mind. I happen to have neural synapses which allow me to process and retain a lot of information quickly. There are others born with different neural synapses, which allow their muscles to have remarkable control and quickness. The human body fascinates me."

"Well, I can assure you that there are some athletically gifted individuals who do try to make other feel inferior," said John. "But I like your perspective."

"Pastor Whitworth warned me about arrogant people. He prepared me for meeting them, and I'm grateful. He's a very interesting man."

"He is," agreed John.

Grady reached down and took one of the flowers from the base of his mother's grave and laid it at the base of the aged grave of Lilly Johnson.

"This grave looks a little lonely," Grady told his father.

292

Chapter 42
Fishing

A gray-haired Mark Fairchild knocked on the door of the cabin owned by his dear friend. Within a moment, the door was answered by a balding man.

"You could have just come inside," said John, fully opening the door. "You've been coming to this cabin for decades."

"You've made that plain to me, before," said Mark. "I just want to make sure that I'm not barging into a situation of you entertaining a hot chick here at the cabin."

"Yeah, right!" John replied with a laugh.

"Well, you never know. You're still a reasonably handsome man, and you're wealthy. I would guess there are plenty of women out there ready to jump your bones."

"You're dreaming," said John. "You're the retired attorney with time on his hands. You're the real catch here."

"Yeah, I hear that sixty is the new forty. But I just don't see it."

"That's because you're sixty-one, not sixty," poked John.

"Don't forget, you're a year older. What's it like

to be totally out of the business of owning properties?”

“Actually, it’s pretty nice. I thought I would miss it, but I don’t.”

“Grady has certainly excelled in the field of medicine,” said Mark. “Did he ever show an interest in the business?”

“No, never. And if I had his mind, I wouldn’t want to waste it on dealing with buying and selling properties. He’s not just one level above me, his mind is in the stratosphere. He’s exactly where God wanted him, if you ask me.”

“Graduating in pre-med at twelve, and med school at fourteen – he is so far out of my league that I feel like a groundhog looking up at the stars. It’s beyond me.”

“I just figured he would be a doctor, but it’s doubtful many patients would want to be treated by a young teen,” said John. “He was wise enough to continue his studies. He became the youngest biomedical research analyst at Harvard University during the same year that he obtained a driver’s license.”

“It’s what he accomplished over the next decade that still blows me away,” said Mark. “I can’t imagine what it feels like to have a kid who cured cancer.”

“Not all forms, just six of them. Besides, Grady didn’t develop the treatments.”

“No, he just showed why those cancer cells morph the way they do,” stated Mark.

“He showed what had to be done to stop the mutation and multiplication of some cancer cells,” said John. “Others developed the treatments.”

“Still, his research was invaluable!”

“True,” agreed John. “That’s why I said that I

believe he is doing exactly what God intended him to do."

"I admire your faith, but why does it have to be something that God is doing? Why can't it be enormous contributions by a remarkable human? It's almost sounds belittling to say that God was using a person to do something. It sort of takes away from the astonishing work of very brilliant people, like Grady."

"Grady is perfectly fine with concept of God working through him."

"For someone with such an enormous intellect, he is remarkably humble," said Mark.

"You'll get no argument from me. However, you came here to fish. I'll make a deal with you."

"What's the deal?"

"I'll fillet the bass, if you'll scale the bream," offered John.

"Only if you skin the catfish."

No catfish were caught, but they reeled in three fair sized smallmouth bass and six bream. Each man kept his side of the bargain, and they sat down to an evening of fish and hush puppies.

"If I remember correctly, Rebecca taught you how to make those hush puppies," said Mark.

"That's right."

"Well, I certainly owe her. There's something special about these things."

"There was something special about Rebecca," said John. "Why didn't you ever marry, Mark?"

"Who says that I won't marry? You never know, the right one may come around any day."

"Right."

"You're the marrying type, John. Why didn't you

remarry? I'm sure it would have helped in raising Grady?"

"It wouldn't have been fair to another woman," answered John. "No other woman could have replaced Rebecca. I don't think I could have hidden that fact, and I don't think it would have been fair to do so."

"I have to ask something."

"Fire away."

"When the FBI presented you all that evidence about that missing girl named Jessica Everett, did you ever think they were right?" asked Mark.

"Not for a minute," answered John.

"You have to admit, Rebecca told a variety of tales about her past. Why couldn't that one be right?"

"I just know that it wasn't. I knew that the woman I married was Rebecca Johnson."

"How could you have been so sure?" asked Mark. "Was it some kind of overwhelming gut feeling? What was it?"

"I trust you, Mark. You've been the best friend any man could ask for. I'm going to show you something. Since Doctor Parker Morgan passed away, only Grady and I know about this."

John rose from his chair, and slowly made his way to the cabin safe. He retrieved an envelope from it, and he removed the contents. Returning to his friend Mark, John handed him papers now yellowed from age.

"I assume these are the infamous papers regarding Danny Moffato," commented Mark.

"No, those were used to start a fire in the fireplace several years ago," replied John. "These are much different."

Chapter 43
Answers

"When Grady was ten-years-old, he asked me why his mother was buried in such a rural cemetery," John told Mark. "I'm about to show you evidence that I shared with my son. I believe the information reported here contributed to Grady's interest in the study of medicine."

John asked him to take a look at lab data and handwritten notes by Doctor Parker Morgan found on the second page.

"Spanish flu?" asked Mark.

John took a seat directly across from the retired attorney.

"After Grady questioned me about the gravesite, he accompanied me to put flowers on Rebecca's grave," John began. "I told him that the cemetery was very special place for his mother. He placed flowers on her grave, and I pulled this document from my jacket pocket and handed it to him."

John recounted the conversation he had with his young son.

"This is a copy of a blood test performed on your mother many years ago," John told Grady. "These papers have been very special to me. While I live, they will remain in that safe. I'll give you the combination, and you may now consider them to be yours."

"I was always told that my mother died in an auto accident," said Grady. "Did she have a terminal illness?"

"The test was done earlier. Note the statement written in the doctor's hand, and the circled finding," answered John.

"It says, Spanish Flu," remarked Grady. "So?"

"The Spanish Flu ended the summer of 1919," answered John. "No one has contracted it since then."

"I don't understand. Why would this say that my mother had signs of having the Spanish Flu?"

"Think about it, Grady. What does this medical record prove?"

"That the Spanish Flu didn't end in 1919?" asked Grady.

"No, it ended in 1919," answered John.

"Well, the other option would be that my mother was around during 1919," Grady said, with a chuckle.

"That's exactly what it means," replied John. "Your mother told me an interesting story before we married. I'm not talking about the story of being bitten by a snake. However, that snake bite incident led your mother to become a patient of my primary physician, Parker Morgan. When she told me that she believed she was pregnant with you, I convinced her to make an appointment with Dr. Morgan. The doctor and I were also friends. I've been a man of means for some time, and I usually find a way to have my questions answered. Prior to your mother's appointment, Parker and I played a round of golf."

"What's golf have to do with a pregnancy test?" asked Grady.

"During the golf outing, I asked Parker how to determine if someone has ever had the Spanish Flu," continued John. "He told me that blood tests can reveal this. I told him that Rebecca had told me about having the Spanish Flu, and that I wanted him to confirm it one way or another. I asked the doctor to take a separate sample of her blood, and have it tested for the Spanish Flu. Of course, he argued that there was no possibility of someone her age ever having the Spanish Flu. But in the end, he decided that it was best for the emotional and mental health of his patient to do as I asked. I swore him to secrecy, and he reminded me that there were laws about spreading personal healthcare data without the patient's consent."

"You didn't tell my mother you were doing this?" asked Grady.

"No, I told her. She and I agreed to always be honest with each other about things. It was the doctor that I was concerned about. So, I convinced him to send the sample in as a blind test, so that her name would not be associated with the testing documentation. He agreed, but was adamant about any signs of flu being the (H1N1)pdm09 virus of 2009, not the H1N1 virus of the Spanish Flu. These papers are the reports of your mother's blood test. Dr, Morgan was floored when he reviewed the results, to say the least. The blood test revealed that she had antibodies consistent with those having the Spanish Flu. It is clinical proof that your mother, at some point in her life, recovered from the Spanish Flu. He thought the findings should be made public, but we convinced him to keep them private. Your mother and I convinced him to make the notations on the test report signifying that these tests were hers. You see the notes, and here is his signature and date of signing."

"I'm not sure that I understand," said Grady.

John told his son of a woman, born in 1896, who had traveled through time and to become his wife. He told him of the FBI and their questions about a pair of murders deep in the Georgia mountains. When their investigations caused them to believe that Rebecca was really Jessica Everett, because of this medical report there was no doubt in John's mind that they were wrong.

"But her grave says that she was born in 1993," stated Grady.

"We had to put that date on the tombstone," explained John. "There would have been no way to explain a birth date of 1896. Also, your mothers Social Security information showed her as being born August 12, 1993."

"All these years, you've hidden this story?" asked Grady.

"Yes, but you're the reason why we had those tests run. Your mother and I had planned to share this information with you when you were grown, but she didn't live to see that. She wanted you to know the truth about her when you were mature enough to understand."

"I can't believe that you hid this all these years," said Grady.

"There's more," replied John. "The little girl buried in the grave beside your mother's is your half-sister, Lilly. Your mother was married to a man before she traveled though time. She miscarried in 1921."

"That explains why she wanted to be buried here!"

"Your mother's first husband was a veteran of the first world war and was a farmer who owned the property where I have the cabin," said John.

"You're kidding me!" shouted Grady. "What else have you hidden from me?"

"Rebecca's husband's name was Grady," answered John.

Grady mouth dropped open. He stood in silence.

"You're not related to him, but I have a picture of your mother and him taken long ago," said John. "It was taken at a ceremony for local World War I veterans. I know this is a lot to take in."

"You have to answer one question," begged Grady.

"I'll answer any question that you have."

"Are you really my father?"

"Absolutely!" exclaimed John. "I have records showing both Rebecca's and my DNA. If you ever need resolution, you're welcome to check yours against ours. You are my only child."

Grady stared at his mother's grave in silence for several moments. He then stooped down and removed one of flowers on Rebecca's grave and placed it on Lilly's.

"This grave looks a little lonely," Grady said.

When John finished the story, it was as if a lightbulb had gone off in Mark's brain.

"I thoroughly misjudged Rebecca," Mark said. "I thought she was a con, who would cause you trouble in life. I apologize. If there is an afterlife, I hope she knows that I'm truly sorry for my lack of trust."

"I believe she's in heaven and that she knows," replied John. "Through my wife, I found a personal faith in God Physical aspects of life can sometimes be explained sufficiently, and more rarely matters of the mind can be understood. However, I'm not really sure that spiritual matters can be logically explained to others. I doubt I would be able to explain this faith to anyone else."

"How do you explain her DNA match with the dead guy in the mountains," asked Mark.

"Rebecca told me that she had a sister. It's possible that the man was a descendent of her sister."

"I feel honored that you would share this with me," said Mark. "I can't say that I share your faith in God, but what you just shared with me is an absolute miracle. It is concrete proof of time travel, and it wasn't by any type of machine. This is unbelievable. I almost feel like I'm dreaming and waiting to wake up."

"Rebecca always wondered why God would cause her to experience the trials resulting from being transported from the year 1922 to the present," John said. "She often told me that she felt that God was angry with her, even possibly cursed by Him. Nevertheless, she maintained her personal faith in Him.

I'm sure she now knows that the genetic mix between the two of us produced a remarkable child. Only a handful of people will come to know this story, but billions will know the results of her journey. While living with me those few years, Rebecca never envisioned that the man who would save so many from cancer would be conceived in this rural cabin by a stream."

304

About the Author

Rob Williams, currently residing in Nacogdoches Texas, has served in multiple roles supporting the Christian community. Included in this long list of mentorships was his service as youth director of an inner-city church in Atlanta and working with children in some of the toughest housing projects in that city. Rob worked at a rehabilitation center for five years, where he became acquainted with the homeless. The center helped those on work release from jail and those who were physically and mentally handicapped. He has taught adult Sunday school classes for more than thirty years and led youth in Boy Scouts and Cub Scouts for twenty years. Retired from the high tech industry in Huntsville Alabama, he writes Christian fiction and science fiction in his free time. Rob is a husband, the father of four, and a grandfather. He is the author of the three novel Brandon Springs Christian fiction series, the dystopian science fiction novel *Sins of Variance*, the Christian fictional crime novel *Gathering of Six*, and Christian mystery *Cabin by the Stream*.